Praise for New York Times *bestselling author Jenn McKinlay's Hat Shop Mysteries*

"Fancy hats and British aristocrats make this my sort of delicious cozy read."

—Rhys Bowen, *New York Times* bestselling author of the Royal Spyness Mysteries

"A delicious romp through my favorite part of London with a delightful new heroine."

—Deborah Crombie, *New York Times* bestselling author

"The sharp writing and smart plotting are outstanding, and the surprising reveal and even more suspenseful chase will have readers at the edge of their seats. This stellar mystery sets a high bar for mysteries."

—Kings River Life Magazine

"Brimming with McKinlay's trademark wit and snappy one-liners, Anglophiles will love this thoroughly entertaining new murder mystery series. A hat trick of love, laughter, and suspense, and another feather in [Jenn McKinlay's] cap."

—Hannah Dennison, author of the Vicky Hill Exclusive! Mysteries

"Delightful." —*Publishers Weekly*

"The mystery itself was captivating, with plenty of red herrings to keep the reader guessing. The resolution was clever and made perfect sense in the end . . . I highly recommend this to those who enjoy all things English and appreciate a strong protagonist." —Open Book Society

"McKinlay has another winner on her hands."

—Fresh Fiction

Berkley Prime Crime titles by Jenn McKinlay

Cupcake Bakery Mysteries

SPRINKLE WITH MURDER
BUTTERCREAM BUMP OFF
DEATH BY THE DOZEN
RED VELVET REVENGE
GOING, GOING, GANACHE
SUGAR AND ICED
DARK CHOCOLATE DEMISE
VANILLA BEANED

Library Lover's Mysteries

BOOKS CAN BE DECEIVING
DUE OR DIE
BOOK, LINE, AND SINKER
READ IT AND WEEP
ON BORROWED TIME
A LIKELY STORY
BETTER LATE THAN NEVER

Hat Shop Mysteries

CLOCHE AND DAGGER
DEATH OF A MAD HATTER
AT THE DROP OF A HAT
COPY CAP MURDER
ASSAULT AND BERET

Jenn McKinlay

BERKLEY PRIME CRIME
New York

BERKLEY PRIME CRIME
Published by Berkley
An imprint of Penguin Random House LLC
375 Hudson Street, New York, New York 10014

ISBN: 9780425279595

First Edition: January 2017

Printed in the United States of America
1 3 5 7 9 10 8 6 4 2

Cover art by Robert Steele
Book design by Laura K. Corless

This one is for you, the readers, who took Scarlett
and Viv and the entire Hat Shop crew into your hearts.
You let me know that you loved reading their stories
as much as I loved writing them, and I am forever
grateful for all of the wonderful e-mails and messages
I received while creating this series.
Thanks so much. You are the best readers *ever*!

Acknowledgments

Hats off to the entire team at Berkley Prime Crime for all of their hard work on this series. Special thanks to Kate Seaver, who loved it from the start; Katherine Pelz, for always taking care of the details; and a big tip of the brim to the art department and illustrator Robert Steele for such lovely book covers. I feel very fortunate to have such talent supporting my stories. Thank you all so much.

An extra thank-you is due to my author friend Dean James, aka Miranda James, for coming up with the clever title *Assault and Beret*. He offered it up a few years ago and while I didn't use it at the time, when this story came along it fit perfectly. Thanks, Dean!

Chapter 1

"You know everyone says that French waiters are rude, but I don't think our waiter is rude at all," I said to my cousin, Vivian Tremont. "He seems very pleasant."

"That's because he's trying to sleep with you, Scarlett," Vivian said. "Why do you think our bottle of La Bodice Cheverny was on the house?"

"Seriously? Free wine for a tussle in the sheets, do I look that easy?" I asked. "Well, that is rude."

"Uh-huh," she said. Which was only slightly better than "I told you so," but not much.

It was late evening in Paris, the City of Light, and we were enjoying a nosh as Viv, who is British, would say. We were seated inside the Bistro Renee on Rue Saint Charles.

The bitter wind that whipped down the smaller streets

from the Seine River could not get us here. We had ducked inside to eat but also to get warm.

Thankfully, the food did not disappoint. I ordered quail with roasted spring onions while Viv indulged in suckling pig with salsify, which is a lot like a parsnip, and we shared a baguette seasoned with the mellow heat of the Espelette pepper from the Basque region, or so our waiter, David, informed us when asked.

He was very charming and quite good-looking with his wavy dark hair and golden eyes. He told us his father owned the bistro, which was named for his mother, Renee, who had passed away when David was just a boy. Honestly, he broke my heart a little with that story but not enough to have a sleepover with him.

The small restaurant was everything a late meal in Paris should be. Candlelight, soft music in the background, an exotic blossom of some sort in a blue bottle on our small square table swathed in a pristine white cloth with matching napkins.

The crumbs of the baguette and the near empty bottle of sauvignon blanc sat on the table between us. We had scraped our plates clean. We did share as only cousins who live together like sisters can with some squabbling over what exactly was equitable and over who had ordered the tastier dish. I had, but Viv refused to admit it because I am her younger American cousin and she refuses to acknowledge that I am just as cultured as she is.

I glanced out the window. It was beautiful but it was not exactly the Paris of my dreams. Instead of sitting on an outside patio enjoying the warm floral-scented breeze of spring, we were swathed in scarves and sweaters, sitting inside a small café watching a January snowfall.

Why were we here? Here's the short version. Viv is an acclaimed London milliner hired to teach a one-week hat-making class at the local art school. I am Scarlett Parker, not just her cousin but also part owner in our millinery business housed on Portobello Road in Notting Hill, London, which we inherited six years ago from our grandmother Mim.

Now because I know you're going to ask, since everyone does, the answer is no, positively, unequivocally no. I can't make a hat to save my life. So what am I doing here with her?

I'm sorry, did you miss the part that we're in Paris? Yes, even in January it's still Paris. Besides, the fact is that while Viv is an amazing artist, she's not the best with people. That's where I come in.

Viv being a creative type is known to occasionally be impulsive. I am generally the voice of reason when this happens but unfortunately when she decided on a whim to elope, she neglected to mention it to me thus I couldn't stop her. This was a couple of years ago while I was busy ruining my own life in a bad relationship.

In hindsight, we were both reeling from the loss of our grandmother Mim and neither of us were making good choices in our grief. Why is hindsight always so much clearer than foresight?

Anyway, after a few weeks of marriage, Viv ditched her husband without properly ending her marriage, and last she knew he was in Paris, so my mission, if I chose to accept it, which I did, was to find her husband and get him to agree to an annulment. Easy peasy, right?

Right. In the meantime, I needed to scrape off our waiter.

"Well, I'm not going to sleep with him," I said. "But I will finish off the wine."

"Naturally," Viv said.

I poured the remainder into our two glasses. Viv raised her glass and I did the same. We gently tapped them together.

"To finding your husband," I said. She blanched.

Okay, that was me being a buzzkill but also keeping her on task. Viv can be sly when she wants to be as evidenced by the fact that she got married and never told me. I mean, honestly, who does that?

"How about to returning home happier than when we arrived," she offered instead.

"I like that," I said. "It leaves it nice and open-ended for all possibilities."

"Precisely," she said.

We drained our glasses.

We declined coffee and a dessert, although I was tempted by the lemon cannoli, and a request for my phone number. In all honesty, I really felt that David must be vision impaired as I have the fiery hair and freckles of my dad's ginger-infused DNA while Viv has the milky complexion and long blond curls of our grandmother. In a beauty competition, Viv beats me hands down every time, yes, even when I put in great effort. Good thing I learned to get by on my personality years ago.

When we stepped outside, the chill wind was relentless, pushing us down the street like we were wayward teenagers being forced home before curfew. I tightened the scarf about my neck and jammed the cuffs of my leather gloves up into the sleeves of my jacket. I really despise the cold.

It was a short walk to Madame Leclaire's apartment building, where the Paris School of Art was housing us for the duration of Viv's class. It was a charming place located on the edge of the fifteenth arrondissement within walking distance of the Eiffel Tower. Built of white stone with a blue mansard roof, it was four stories tall containing eight small apartments with the added bonus of a communal living room and dining room on the main floor, where Madame Leclaire served a continental breakfast every day and a nightcap in the evenings.

The furniture in our apartment was a mashup of antiques with modern accessories. We each had a twin bed and a large armoire in our rooms, which were connected by a sitting room with a kitchenette. We were on one of the upper floors and our apartment had large windows with narrow wrought iron balconies. Mostly, our view was of the similar building across the way and the street below, but if I pressed my body against the glass and angled my head just right, I could glimpse a sliver of the Eiffel Tower to the north of us.

The house was warm and safe and Madame Leclaire, who ran it, was lovely and charming and always seemed to have the best wine and cheese on hand. That is a wonderful quality in an apartment building owner.

With our scarves wrapped around our heads, conversation

was impossible as we hurried down the street. The snow was getting sharper as it pelted my back, pushing me toward my fluffy soft bed. I really didn't need the encouragement.

The lights were on in the front room of Madame Leclaire's. Viv and I picked up our pace. We dashed up the steps and hurried into the vestibule. Viv pressed the intercom and called a cheery, "Hello, we're home."

We had a key, but if Madame Leclaire was about, we could use the intercom and she would buzz us in. The inside door opened with a *click* and we pushed through with the eagerness of schoolgirls looking for cookies after a long day. Warmth washed over us and Madame Leclaire popped her head out of the communal sitting room on the first floor.

"Girls, you look frozen, you should come and sit by the fire." She gestured for us to follow her. Honestly, with her alluring French accent, I would have followed her anywhere, but the fire seemed like an excellent suggestion.

We did not need to be asked twice. Well, Viv might have, she's British, and they do hem and haw a lot in a show of good manners, but I am American and I do not. I walked right into the cozy room without hesitation and plopped myself in a darling chair right in front of the fire.

"This is heaven," I said. I peeled off my short wool coat and let the heat from the flames wash over me.

"Would you care for some hot chocolate?" Madame Leclaire offered. "Usually, I serve something stronger in the evening, but with the snow, I felt like chocolate was most appropriate."

"Oh, we don't want to trouble you," Viv said at the same time I said, "Yes, please."

Madame Leclaire glanced between us and smiled, amused no doubt by how different we were. She was much too polite to say so, however.

Madame was tall and lithe, with a cap of dark curls about her heart-shaped face that were just beginning to go gray. Her lips were wide and generous and her eyes a rich, trustworthy brown. I had liked her immediately when we arrived the day before, and she had been nothing but gracious and kind to us, which just reinforced my first impression.

This evening she wore tailored black slacks and a crisp raspberry blouse, which was mostly covered by the charcoal gray cashmere wrap she had draped about her shoulders, giving her a look that was both chic and comfy at the same time. You simply cannot outdress the French, and I would never be stupid enough to try.

Viv perched on the edge of the seat across from mine as if getting ready to bail the moment she felt her presence was an imposition. I burrowed deeper into my chair.

A silver pot with a random collection of mismatched china cups sat on the table in front of the couch, where Madame Leclaire resumed her seat. A cup of half-drunk chocolate sat on a coaster and beside it a French novel was facedown on the highly polished wooden table.

Now I wondered if we had intruded upon Madame Leclaire's quiet time. But I thought not, because the other cups on the tray indicated that she was open to company.

As if she was reading my thoughts, she took a delicate china cup and poured the piping hot chocolate into it. She placed it on a mismatched saucer and handed it to me. The steam rising out of the cup smelled a little like I've always imagined heaven would smell, assuming of course that there is one and that I am invited.

Madame Leclaire looked at Viv as if trying to determine if she wanted chocolate or if she was about to flee the room.

"Yes?" she asked as she held up the pot.

"Thank you, Madame Leclaire," Viv said. "You are most kind."

"Please call me Suzette," she said. "Most of my tenants do."

"Most?" I asked. "Which ones don't?"

"The ones I don't like," she said.

Viv and I both laughed at the wicked gleam in her eye.

"We are very honored that you like us," I said. Then I added, "Suzette."

Viv sipped her hot chocolate and I saw her spine relax as she melted into her chair. There really is nothing a good cup of cocoa can't cure.

"You start your class tomorrow?" Suzette asked.

"Yes, bright and early," Viv said. "Monsieur Martin said he would be by to escort me."

"He is very attentive," Suzette said. "Do you both teach millinery or do you teach something different, Ms. Parker?"

"Scarlett, please," I said.

"And I'm Vivian, or Viv, if you prefer," Viv chimed in.

"I don't teach anything," I said. "I have no artistic ability at all. The last hat I tried to make looked like a very bad brioche."

Suzette covered her mouth with one delicate hand and laughed. "I am sure that is not true."

"Oy, it's true," Viv said with the candor only a cousin could manage without it being a slam to the ego.

"What will you do with your time then, Scarlett, while Viv is teaching?"

"I am going to be looking for her husband," I said.

Viv gasped and Suzette's perfectly arched eyebrows rose almost to her hairline. Even surprise looked good on her.

"I am afraid I do not comprehend," Suzette said. "You are looking for a husband for your cousin?"

"No, I'm actually looking for *her* husband," I said. "She misplaced him."

Viv glowered at me and I shrugged.

"What?" I asked. "You did. Besides, maybe Suzette can help me figure out where to start."

"But of course, if there is anything I can do to help, I will do so gladly," she said.

"See?" I said to Viv. She continued glowering at me and I was pretty sure she growled deep in her throat but then she sipped her cocoa and seemed to settle back down again.

"But do explain to me how you misplace a husband," Suzette said. She smiled over the edge of her own cup. "I may need to know how to do that one day."

Chapter 2

Our apartment was cold. I burrowed deeper under my thick duvet, trying to ignore the pale light coming through my window. It couldn't be morning yet, I refused to accept it.

I had almost drifted back to sleep when the door to my bedroom crashed open and Viv came dashing into the room.

"Scarlett, wake up," she cried. "I need to talk to you."

No, no, no! I clenched my eyes tight, refusing to be ordered about when I was unconscious and trying to remain that way. I didn't move, hoping if she thought I was dead asleep, or perhaps plain old dead, she would go away.

My covers were abruptly yanked off my body, exposing my flannel pajamas with the yellow rubber ducks on them to the crisp morning air. I yelped and scrambled to pull them back over me, although I wasn't sure if it was the cold or the embarrassment over my sleeping attire that made me move faster.

Viv wasn't having it, however, and maintained her grip, forcing me into a tug of war over my own blankets.

"Viv! Stop it!" I cried. "I'm going to freeze to death and it will be all your fault."

"Then pay attention, because I need you to make me a promise," she said. "Wait. What are you wearing?"

"Rubber duckies and they were a Christmas present from my parents. They're cute so don't be snarky," I said.

"Me?" She blinked at me.

"You. Now, what's the promise?"

Honestly, I'd have agreed to shave my head and learn to play the bagpipes at that point as my teeth were chattering and goose bumps were rising on any exposed skin, but I knew better than to give my cousin a blind promise. I had done it last year and found myself wearing a hat that looked like a big pickle at one of the biggest social events of the season. Mortifying.

Viv let go of her corner of the blankets and I fell back against my pillow and yanked the duvet up around my ears. Ah, blessed warmth.

Viv was already showered and dressed and looking very professorial in a fitted gray tweed blazer with black suede elbow patches over a blue turtleneck sweater. Her long blond curls were tamed into a thick braid that hung over her shoulder. She wore a knee-length black skirt and black boots that molded to her calves but were low-heeled enough for a long day on her feet.

"You look very pretty," I said. I glanced at the clock. "And you're disgustingly on time."

"Thanks," she said. "Monsieur Martin will be here shortly and I don't want to keep him waiting. Listen, when you get up, I think you should take the day off. There's no rush in finding William, and who knows, he could have forgotten all about me by now."

I peeked at her from behind the blanket. "He married you. I doubt he's forgotten you."

"Maybe. Still I want you to promise me that you won't make contact with him without telling me first."

I shook my head. I was so glad I hadn't agreed to such a ridiculous promise.

"It's been almost two years. Possibly he had the marriage annulled and the whole thing is a moot point," she said. "So there's no need to bother him."

I shook my head again.

"Or he could be dead," she said. "Not that I think that's an acceptable outcome, but it might have—"

I shook my head again. "That didn't happen," I said.

"You don't know—"

"Yeah, I do," I said. "Look, I didn't want to say anything because I didn't want to spook you, but I had our friend Inspector Simms do some digging. Your husband, Mr. William Graham, is alive and well and living here in Paris just as you suspected."

"Where?" she asked. Her bright blue eyes, one of the few features we shared, went round and she glanced from side to side as if she expected him to jump out at her from the shadows.

"I don't know," I said. "I called the place listed as his last known address and they said he had moved out with no forwarding address."

"That's odd, don't you think?" she asked.

"Maybe," I said. I bit my lip. I hadn't wanted to have this discussion until after I found him but maybe this was for the best. "It could be that he has moved in with someone and didn't think to leave a forwarding address."

"Oh, God." Viv slumped across the bed. My shins had to be digging into her back but she was apparently too distraught to care. "Maybe he left no information because he was afraid that I was going to come looking for him. Maybe he is hiding out from me. What am I going to do? This was a terrible idea. I can't face him. He likely hates me."

"I don't think he knows you well enough to hate you," I said. "How long were you two together?"

"Six weeks," she said.

"Yeah, he never got to see the real you. Trust me, there is no hatred there, confusion undoubtedly, but no hatred," I said.

"Apathy, then," she said. "After all, if he doesn't hate me, why didn't he come after me?"

"Because you ditched him?" I guessed. "If anything, I'll bet he thinks you hate him."

"That's awful!" Viv cried. "He must think me a complete nutter. How can I face him?"

"Really?" I asked. "That never occurred to you before?"

"Well, no," she said.

And that right there is the difference between me and Viv. She has an inability to think about how her actions affect others, whereas I spend most of my time thinking about making people happy. It's the hospitality industry thing, you know, making sure people have what they need when they need it, turning every interaction with a customer into a positive experience.

Frankly, it's an exhausting line of work, but I've discovered that partnering with my artistic cousin, who tends to follow her own artistic whims instead of the desires of her customers, really lets me exercise that people-pleasing muscle. I've had to talk more than one woman out of shanking Viv with a hat pin when the hat Viv created for them was, perhaps, not quite what they were expecting. Good times.

"And that is precisely why you need to let me make contact with him first," I said. "I can make sure there are no hard feelings, grudges, or hits put out on anyone involved in your brief go at matrimony."

"A hit?" Viv frowned. "That seems overly dramatic."

"I was joking," I assured her. I glanced at the clock. "Don't you need to meet Mr. Martin now?"

"Oh, drat." Viv blew out an exasperated breath as she sat up. "Call me when you find him. I mean it, Scarlett. I want to talk to you before you talk to him."

"That I can do," I said. I pulled the covers up over my head. "Now go away."

Suzette was in the front room when I made my way downstairs. It looked as if she was just cleaning up from breakfast.

"Good morning, Scarlett, did you sleep well?" she asked.

Today she was wearing a bright red sweater over gray wool pants and stylish black suede half boots. She looked more like an executive than a bed-and-breakfast owner. Curious.

"I did, thank you," I said.

"*Café*?" she asked.

"Please," I said. "Sorry I missed breakfast."

"Not at all," she said. She placed a steaming cup of coffee down beside me with a small silver pitcher of steamed milk. "Your cousin had me put aside two *pain aux raisins* for you. She assured me that is what you would have chosen for yourself."

"*Viennoiserie*?" I sat up straighter.

"*Oui*," she said.

She turned to a sideboard, groaning with empty dishes, and brought back a plate covered in a blue and white cloth. When she took off the cloth, I might have wept a little.

One of the things I love most about Paris is the breakfast pastry also called *viennoiserie*. As you might have guessed, I have a small bread problem, okay, bread and cheese problem, all right, it's really a bread, cheese, and wine problem. Heck, I should probably just move to Paris.

Pain aux raisins is a swirl of flaky pastry with raisins tucked inside. Its buttery goodness melts in your mouth and goes perfectly with a cup of hot coffee. To say I was in heaven was not an overstatement.

What I learned on a trip to Paris several years before

was the distinction between a *boulangerie*, a bread bakery, and a *patisserie*, a dessert bakery. The *viennoiserie*, which hovers somewhere between bread and pastry with its sweetened breads like the *pain aux chocolate*, is by far my favorite of all the delicious baked goods to be found in Paris and can usually be found in both.

Viennoiserie is the style of Viennese pastry making. Turns out, the Austrians made the croissant first and brought it to Paris in 1770 when Austrian princess Marie Antoinette married King Louis XVI. The French bakers made the crescent moon–shaped pastries to honor her and then perfected them, making the croissant one of the most popular foods associated with France.

Suzette sat down across from me while I tried to savor each bite of flaky pastry and resist the urge to stuff the whole thing in my mouth. She smiled at me as if she knew it was a struggle to maintain my good manners.

"Monsieur Martin seemed very excited to have Vivian as a teacher," Suzette said. "I believe this is the first time that his art school has offered hat making."

"Viv will do a wonderful job," I said.

I wondered if she heard the lack of confidence in my voice and I forced a smile to try and hide it. Judging by the way she tipped her head to study me, I was pretty sure I failed.

It wasn't that I didn't think Viv could teach the class. I knew she could. It was just that the search for her husband was bound to make her more distracted than usual and Viv operated in a constant state of creative distraction as it was, so I was feeling cautiously optimistic about the class at best. Mostly, I was hoping it would keep her occupied and out of my hair while I tracked down her husband.

"So, what's your backstory?" I asked Suzette. I was desperate for a change of subject and she intrigued me.

Her perfectly arched eyebrows rose on her forehead, not even causing a wrinkle. She really did have remarkable skin.

"Backstory?" she asked. "Do you mean my life story?"

"Yes, your history," I said. "I don't mean to be rude, but you don't carry yourself like a landlord."

"I don't?"

"No, I don't see you as a bucket-and-mop sort of woman so much as I see an executive," I said. "A businesswoman."

"Running this place is a business," she countered.

"Yes, but you walk with a certain authority," I said. "I get the feeling that you were the boss of many people at one time."

A small smile tipped the corners of her lips. "You are very astute, Scarlett. One might say that you walk with the same purpose and yet you work in a *petite* hat shop."

"Very true." I laughed. "All right, I'll show you mine if you show me yours."

She frowned and I realized I really had to cut back on the slang or pick up some French slang pronto.

"I used to work in the hotel industry in Florida," I said. "I managed a resort hotel with over one hundred employees."

She pressed the tip of her index finger to her lower lip and tapped it while she considered me. The look she gave me was sharp. She was the sort of person who didn't miss much.

"You are the party crasher, *oui*?" she asked. "The girl on the Internet who threw cake at the man who told her he was single but was still married."

"Ugh." I groaned and dropped my chin to my chest. Someday, somehow, surely, I would leave behind my embarrassing past. Then again, they said that once something went viral on the Internet, it lived forever. Perhaps I just needed to embrace it.

When I glanced up, she was biting her lower lip and trying not to laugh.

"You know, people keep telling me that I will find that incident funny someday, but I'm still waiting," I said.

"I'm sorry," she said. "I am not laughing at you, truly."

"I know," I said. "Now that my ex has been outed for his philandering, most people are laughing at him, as they should. But I dated him for so long and the whole time I thought he was separated and well on the way to divorce. I never would have gotten involved with him had I known. I don't think I will ever forget thc feeling of having my heart crushed when I walked into the reception hall of the hotel I managed for his family and found him with his wife, having an enormous anniversary party."

"What a bastard," she said.

"I prefer rat bastard," I said. Then I smiled. "Of course, the look on his face when I threw that cake at him and nailed him, well, that has taken on a fuzzy, romantic glow for me."

I laughed and she joined me.

"If it is any consolation, you made every woman who has ever been lied to or cheated on very happy. You took revenge for us all," she said.

"You sound as if you have some understanding of the situation," I said.

"You were right before, about me," she said. "I was an executive for Magnifique, but I had to leave."

"Magnifique, the cosmetics company?" I asked.

She nodded. I was silent. I didn't want to pressure her into sharing if she wasn't ready.

"My boss . . ." She paused and I couldn't help myself.

"You had an affair with your boss?" I asked. Boy, did I get that one.

She shook her head. "No, I had an affair with my boss's husband."

"Oh," I said.

"He assured me that their marriage was over and he was just waiting for the right time to tell her," she said. "I was stupid and believed him. She found out and I was fired."

"I am so sorry," I said.

She shrugged. "It is no more than I deserved. When we think with our hearts instead of our heads, it seldom turns out well."

"And sometimes it really sucks," I said.

She laughed and I knew we both felt better for sharing our mutual shame. It made the burden lighter somehow.

"And now you are off to look for your cousin's

husband," she said. "I hope he proves worthy of the trouble."

I lifted my cup in a silent salute. I hadn't said anything to Viv, or anyone else for that matter, but I had serious reservations about William Graham. A man who just let his wife walk away and never made any attempt to find her had to have some serious issues of his own, right?

Chapter 3

Viv, being Viv, was not a fountain of information on her husband. She knew his name, William Graham, his occupation, insurance investigator, and that he was an American living in Paris. She did not have a photo of him, an e-mail, or a telephone number.

I had done several Internet searches on him and had found nothing—the guy wasn't on any sort of social media, and the name "William Graham" brought up hundreds of men by that name but the only one in Paris was an accountant in Paris, Texas, who was seventy-five years old. I was pretty confident that this wasn't our guy.

After the public spectacle of my breakup, I had made my Internet footprint as small as possible, so I understood that not everyone wanted to live their life online for public consumption. Then again, I had decided to fly under the radar because of the humiliation of being labeled the party crasher, so what was William Graham hiding from? Vivian? Or was he just antisocial by nature?

Even my friend Detective Inspector Simms of the Metropolitan Police Department hadn't managed to dig up anything other than a last-known address in Paris for him with the flimsy information Viv supplied. I tried to console myself that at least William Graham wasn't a wanted serial killer; even so, with almost no knowledge of him or his life, Viv had married him. It boggled.

But this was Viv. When I had first landed in London, arriving on the ticket she had sent me when she insisted that I needed to get out of the States, I had been greeted by our business manager, Harrison Wentworth, or Harry as I liked to call him, because Viv was missing. So, the marrying on a whim thing, yeah, so Viv.

Thinking about Harry made me feel a pang in my chest. I missed him. He was more than just our business manager to me. He was the guy I was determined would be my boyfriend as soon as I lifted my ban on dating, which was coming up in just a couple months.

Why did I have a ban on dating? Well, my British mother in her very polite but cutting way had pointed out after my party crasher humiliation that perhaps I might take a break from dating for a year. Yes, a whole year. It was a bold maneuver for me as, up until then, I had never gone more than two weeks without a boyfriend.

That sounds worse than it is, really. It's just that I'm a very social person and I like boys, clearly. I mean, who doesn't want to be taken out to dinner rather than sitting at home? Yes, one could argue that I have a problem being alone, but hey, I am ten months into this single thing and I've gotten pretty good at it, thank you very much. I mean, babies had been conceived and born in the time that I had been single.

Whoa, that made me want to sit down and I would have, except I was outside walking to the nearest train station, and it was really freaking cold as the wind whipped down the street, curving its icy fingers into the collar of my wool coat as if it could freeze my skin with just its touch.

Getting around Paris wasn't really much different than London. We have the Underground; they have the Metro. One of the very first things I did when we arrived was to buy my Metro pass, since I used mine so much in London I would have felt naked without it.

Their Metro seemed a little more complicated, with two different train systems, than the Underground, but I was certain it was because I wasn't used to it. Viv and I were staying in 15ème, or the fifteenth arrondissement, called Parc des Expositions. The city of Paris is made up of twenty such arrondissements, like districts or neighborhoods, which were numbered and spiraled out from the center, with the Louvre and the Palais Royale being in the first, the very center of the city.

Suzette had graciously pointed me in the direction of the station that I needed to get from the fifteenth to the first. I was confident that I could figure it out even if it meant I went the wrong way once or twice and had to double back. This was the beauty of not having a schedule. I had all the time in the world to find my way, and I was sure that I would enjoy every bit of it, and if I had to pop in at a local patisserie to get warm, so be it.

I tightened my scarf and hurried toward Dupleix, the aboveground station for the 6 line. Judging by Suzette's directions, this was the shortest way from our place on the Left Bank over to the Right Bank, where I'd pick up the 1 line that would take me to my destination. I could switch trains one more time and make the trip shorter, but I loved riding the elevated 6 line, especially when we crossed over the Seine River and got a spectacular view of the Eiffel Tower. It made my heart lift in my chest every time.

After careful consideration, I had decided the best way to hunt down William Graham was to go to the source, the big baddy, the Louvre. Surely the largest museum in the city if not the world had to have some connection to a company that specialized in insuring art.

Yes, that is about all Viv knew about William Graham's business, that he had been an art major with delusions of being an artist, but when he got to Paris, he'd ended up insuring great works of art instead of painting them. Life is a journey, I suppose.

The train wasn't overly crowded and the trip was short. I did go the wrong way twice, but that was mostly because the Charles de Gaulle–Étoile Station was massive with both Metro and RER trains coming and going, and I think I was hungry. A person can't be responsible for bad decisions when they are hungry. I believe this all the way down to my squishy, hungry middle. Plus, I have a horrible sense of direction.

It was midday by the time I got to the Palais Royale Metro stop near the Louvre, and even though last night's snow had melted and it was the middle of January and cold outside, there were still plenty of tourists. It didn't appear that Mona Lisa and I would be spending any quality alone time together but I had expected as much.

Unlike the National Gallery in London, which is free, the Louvre costs nine and a half euros. I figured it was worth it to go into what is arguably the greatest museum in the world and, yeah, to find a clue as to Viv's husband's whereabouts. I had bought an advance ticket, to avoid the line at the pyramid, which was another wonderful thing about the Louvre. It has multiple entrances, so it is possible to avoid long lines if you plan accordingly.

The entrance to the Musée du Louvre was a real jaw dropper. I went in the Passage Richelieu from Rue de Rivoli and peeked into the huge courtyard in which sat the famous glass pyramid. It was huge and beckoned visitors forth as if it had a magnetic pull.

Honestly, I don't see how a person could just walk by and not investigate. Being the curious sort, I walked right up to the water feature surrounding it and studied the structure under the gray midday light.

Diamond panes of glass made up the pyramid, and as I watched, a bride and groom climbed up onto the cement edge of the pool and posed for a photographer who stood below them. The pyramid loomed behind them, and even though the bride was shivering, I could tell the pictures were going to be amazing. It was the Louvre; how could they not be?

A bitter wind blew through the courtyard, encouraging me to get moving. I wasn't sure where the curators' offices were, but I knew that's who I wanted to speak with, at least to start.

I turned back into the Passage Richelieu and entered the museum. The Richelieu entrance is one of the best-kept secrets for hacking the lines at the Louvre. You're welcome.

The time on my phone told me it was early. On Monday, the museum didn't close until six in the evening, giving me several hours. Wandering the galleries and looking at the art was too good of an opportunity to pass up since I didn't know when I'd get back here again.

I wasn't much of an artist but that didn't mean I didn't appreciate it. Mim had taken Viv and me to Paris several times when we were young, and she had shared her love of still-life paintings with us. I knew that seeking out our favorite piece, an eighteenth-century piece called *Still Life with Figs* by Melendez, would bring her close to me. Without hesitation, I headed in that direction.

It had been several years since Mim had passed, and I still missed her like crazy. I missed the way she always smelled faintly of lily of the valley, and how I could tell her anything and she always took my side, even when I was wrong. I missed the way her bright blue eyes, the color and shape of which both Viv and I had inherited, sparkled when she was getting up to mischief, and I missed the way her hugs could make everything better.

Decision made, I set off to see the Spanish paintings in Room 30. I glanced at the other pieces on the walls on my way, appreciating them but not lingering. Tourists still wearing their coats and the headsets the museum provided for their own walking tour clustered around certain pieces and then moved on. I navigated my way around them until I reached the area I wanted.

When I arrived, I discovered the room was cordoned off and several museum workers were rearranging the pieces of art. I tried to swallow my disappointment. Of all the sections of the museum, why did it have to be this one that was getting made over?

I turned to go and noticed that an official-looking person, a woman in a pencil skirt with her hair in a sleek updo, was directing the workers. She had to be a curator overseeing the process. I moved closer. Maybe she could help me in my search for William Graham.

"Well, all right, Mim," I whispered. If it hadn't been for Mim sharing her love of still-life works with me, I never would have come here first. I waited for the smell of lily of the valley to tickle my nose.

There was nothing but the cold astringent museum smell assaulting my nostrils. I tried not to feel disappointed. I know it sounds crazy but both Viv and I have had moments where we were quite certain that the essence of Mim was still with us and we were sure we could smell her lily of the valley perfume when it happened. Mental, I know.

I approached the stanchion rope, trying to see past it to the room beyond. Maybe I'd get a glimpse of the painting or the woman's attention; either one was good.

"I'm sorry, Ma'am, this section is closed," a security officer said. He was in uniform and his English was impeccable. I wondered how many different languages he spoke and wondered why he assumed English was my native tongue. I mean, he was right, but still. I shook my head. I didn't want to stray off my mission.

"Is that woman the curator of this collection?" I asked.

"Ms. Harvey?" he asked. "No, she's the assistant to Dr. Pilson. He's over there."

He pointed out an austere-looking gentleman leaning against the wall behind me. He held one arm across his middle with his elbow resting on his fist while he stroked his gray beard with his other hand. He had pointy features and big, thick, round glasses. He reminded me a bit of an owl.

"Thanks," I said to the guard. "I'll ask him."

I crossed the hallway and held my hand out. "Dr. Pilson? Hi, I'm Scarlett Parker."

He blinked behind the glasses. He didn't take my hand, leaving me to awkwardly put my hand on my hip as if I'd meant to do that all along.

"I was wondering if I might ask you some questions."

"No."

"Excuse me?"

"No, go away." His accent was thick and brusque. I couldn't place it, but his meaning was more than clear. He blinked at me and repeated, "Go away."

Now I'd met my share of rudesby folks in my day, but this guy was rocketing to the top of my list of people I wanted to slap, really hard.

"I—" I began but he interrupted.

"What do you not understand about the word 'no'?" he shouted. Spittle flew out of his mouth as he threw up his hands in complete disgust.

Everyone in the hallway and the room beyond came to a complete standstill. All the better to witness my utter humiliation, I suppose.

"I understand," I snapped. "I was about to apologize for interrupting you, you big butthead."

His beard quivered as his eyes narrowed behind his glasses. He was clenching his hands into fists, and for a second, I really thought he was going to strike me.

"Dr. Pilson, I'll take care of this." A woman's voice brought his attention from me as he glanced over my shoulder at the speaker and nodded.

I turned to find the woman with the updo, Ms. Harvey, standing behind us. I could tell from her voice that she was an American. I know it sounds lousy, but this made me feel better, as if being an American, she might be more on my side than her boss's. Dumb, I know.

"Make her go," Dr. Pilson ordered.

"Yes, sir," she said.

He strode past us into the roped-off area without a backward glance. It took everything I had not to kick him in the patoot as he went.

"Follow me," the woman said. She looked as pinched up as Dr. Pilson, and I wondered if I was about to get tossed out a back door into the cold. I've been kicked out of a few places in my time, my ex's anniversary party being one, but being chucked from a museum was a whole new low. Awesome.

Ms. Harvey led the way down a corridor marked *Employes Seulement*. My French wasn't great but even I knew this meant Staff Only. Despite the narrow skirt, Ms. Harvey had a long-legged gait that I had to admire. I imagined she was used to all eyes being on her, and she didn't hurry her steps, allowing everyone to look their fill.

She had a grace and style that was enviable, like most of the Parisians I'd seen, very poised and self-assured. Since she was an American, I wondered how long she had been in Paris and how long it had taken her to acquire that trait. Maybe the French taught lessons in school on how to enter a room. Lord knew, I could have used those as a kid.

Ms. Harvey unlocked an old wooden door and pushed it open. She gestured for me to go first and I stepped inside. It was a tiny, cluttered office not much bigger than a closet, and I had to turn sideways so that she could maneuver around me to get to her desk.

She gestured for me to take the lone hard wooden chair shoved up against the wall while she sat at her desk. There was a narrow window behind her that let in just enough wintery gray light that she didn't have to put on her desk lamp. Stacks of folders and papers filled all of the available desk space, much like the floor-to-ceiling bookcases that surrounded the room were crammed tight, looking like they wanted to belch to relieve the pressure.

"I'm sorry about Dr. Pilson," she said. Her voice was low and deep and matched her wide-set eyes, pointy chin, and jutting cheekbones perfectly. Honestly, if there was an ugly person in Paris, I had yet to meet them. "He can be very . . ."

"Cranky?" I supplied.

She smiled. Then she looked down at her desk and I saw her shoulders shake. She was laughing.

"You called him a butthead," she said. When she glanced up, tears of mirth were coursing down her cheeks. "My goodness, that was fabulous."

"I take it he's your boss," I said.

"One of them," she said. "I'm an assistant to several of the curators, who despite their idiosyncrasies, are the world's most knowledgeable people in their specific fields."

"So, there's some ego," I said. "Being the best of the best and all."

"A lot with some and a touch with others, and with a few rare treasures, none at all," she agreed. "But I am guessing you are not here to discuss the manners of the curators."

"Correct," I said. "I am actually looking for some information about insuring artwork."

"And you came here?"

"It seemed like a good starting place." I shrugged.

"I suppose that depends upon what you need, um, I'm sorry I didn't catch your name," she said.

"Scarlett. Scarlett Parker, from London," I said.

She gave me a look as if to say, *You don't sound like a Londoner.*

"From London most recently," I clarified. "I grew up mostly in the States."

She nodded as if this made sense. "I'm Michelle Harvey, from Boston originally, but I've been here about ten years now."

"I love Boston. My parents live in Briar Creek, Connecticut," I said. "Truly, we're practically neighbors."

We smiled at each other. See? It is a bond being a foreigner in a foreign land.

"What can I do for you, Scarlett?"

"I'm looking for a man," I said.

Her perfectly arched eyebrows rose just enough to let me know that my statement had been unexpected.

"And by that, I mean a man who works in the art world as an insurance agent of sorts," I said. "Given that the Louvre is the center of the art world in Paris, I thought you might have heard of him."

"Perhaps, what is his name?"

"William Graham," I said.

Michelle's expression didn't change but a stillness came over her that I found interesting.

"May I ask why?" she asked.

Now here was a conundrum I hadn't really thought through. I didn't want to say because he was married to my cousin Viv since I had no idea how he was living his life here in Paris. What if he had a girlfriend or two? It could be disastrous.

"My cousin, Vivian Tremont, is a milliner in London," I said. I paused to see if there was a flicker of recognition for Viv's name. She was quite the sensation in the UK, after all. There wasn't. Damn Americans, why didn't they pick up the hat thing? "We own a shop together called Mim's Whims in Notting Hill."

She glanced at me curiously as if this was a strange amount of backstory to be offering. I agreed, but since I was stalling to make my tale seem more plausible, I didn't have much choice.

"Viv has been approached by a museum to create hats for a history of fashion installation," I said. Sometimes even I am stunned at my ability to lie when required. "The value of the collection will be irreplaceable to us and I was told that this Mr. Graham would be able to help us insure the hats."

Michelle considered me for a moment. "I'm not sure Mr. Graham is the exact man you need, but an underwriter in the company he works for, O'Toole Insurance, should be able to help you."

She pulled out her phone and scrolled through her contacts. When she found the name she sought, she turned the display screen so I could see it. There was the name "O'Toole Insurance" and the address. I was so happy I could have burst into song, but singing isn't really my gift so I decided to spare us both and just snapped a picture of the information with my own phone.

"Thank you so much," I said. "You've been a huge help."

"You're welcome," she said. "Good luck with your installation. Let me know when it goes up. I'd love to see it. Although I don't wear them, I've always had a fascination for hats."

"I will," I said. She walked me back to the main hallway and pointed me in the direction of the exit. It had been quite the stroke of luck to run into her, almost too lucky, and I paused to see if I smelled any lily of the valley. I didn't and I felt woefully disappointed. It was ridiculous, I knew that, but grief makes a person hope for all sorts of crazy things.

I thought about spending the rest of the day at the Louvre, but I really couldn't afford the time. We only had one week to locate William Graham and get him to agree to an annulment. If everything went as easily as it should, I figured I could come back to the museum before we left for London.

Part of me did not want to go back out into the cold. I didn't like the way it made my hair crackle with static and my nose run. It had been in the high thirties and low forties—that would be three to five degrees for the Celsius folks—since we had arrived. I knew that January was the coldest and wettest month in France, but just because I was mentally prepared did not mean my toes were. I hugged my wool coat closer and tightened my scarf. This was misery.

As I slogged out of the courtyard of the museum, I tried to imagine what the Louvre was like when it was the royal palace. What would it be like to live in such a vast space? I couldn't even wrap my head around it. The chill in my bones took hold, and I sped up my pace, hoping to warm up with the exercise.

To think that a year ago, I had been managing the crown

jewel in the exclusive Santiago hotel and resort chain in Tampa, Florida. My days were all miniskirts and sandals with pretty blouses and sunhats. I'd had a huge staff to manage and I did it very well. My boss, also my boyfriend, yes, I know that was my first bad choice, assured me that he saw great things in my future.

Of course, I never should have gotten involved with Carlos Santiago. Of Cuban descent, he was handsome, suave, charming, debonair, all of that, and my stupid twenty-five-year-old heart hadn't stood a chance. When he hired me, he was just separating from his wife, or so he said.

You know that joke? The old "that's what she said" plopped onto anything with a bit of sexual innuendo, yeah, it's hilarious. But in my experience the female equivalent would be, "or so he said." I don't think one thing that came out of Carlos Santiago's mouth had ever been the truth, not that he was separated, not that he was getting a divorce, and most definitely not that he loved me.

I sighed. In any event, I don't think a year ago anyone could have foreseen me tracking down my cousin's missing husband on a frigid day in January in Paris. But wasn't that what was so great about life? You never really knew what direction it was going to take.

Michelle told me that the distance between the museum and the office I was looking for was walkable. As the chill wind slapped my hair across my face and the steel gray clouds above clenched their cumulus fists, promising rain, I was not so sure.

I passed the Saint-Germain l'Auxerrois, a massive gray stone church, which was the parish church of the royal family when the Louvre was their palace. It loomed overhead, and when I glanced up, I saw several gargoyles glaring down at me or perhaps trying to spit on me, hard to say.

Either way, they were pretty cool. I decided right then that all buildings should have gargoyles, and I wondered what Viv would think about putting some on Mim's Whims. She was artsy so it could go either way.

We already had an enormous wardrobe that sat in the corner of the shop with a large wooden raven with wings splayed carved on the top. I had nicknamed him Ferd the Bird, and I swear he understood when I spoke to him, which I did frequently.

Viv, bless her heart, only poked a little fun at my contentious relationship with Ferd. Mostly, he and I got on just fine, but there were days when I was quite sure he was mocking me.

So, really, a couple of gargoyles on the eaves would fit right in, right? Yeah, I probably needed to work on that argument a bit more. I was clutching my phone in my gloved hands and I had to check it repeatedly to make certain I was going in the right direction.

The sidewalks were fairly clear. The usual throngs clogging up the walkways that one usually stumbled around in the City of Light were clearly hiding out in bistros or art galleries or napping, which was what I would be doing if I were given the choice. I trudged on.

A right turn here, a left turn there, a run across Rue de

Whatever, and voilà! I rounded a corner and there in front of me was a three-story brick building with a wrought iron gate. The pinpoint on my phone was pointing right to it.

I glanced at the door and saw a small brass plaque that read *O'Toole Insurance*. It appeared I had arrived.

Chapter 4

I was feeling pretty optimistic about things as I opened the gate and strode up the small flight of stairs to the austere brick building that loomed above me. If things kept going this smoothly, I might even find some time to do some shopping in Paris. Now if that didn't warm my girlish heart, nothing would.

The front door was locked. I wondered if this was normal or if it was one of the many subtle changes to life after the attacks in Paris. Yes, people carried on with their lives after suffering through an act of terrorism, but there were always subtle changes that marked the end of the way of life as it had been.

I scanned the wall for a doorbell or a buzzer. A tiny button was seated in a decorative tile. I pressed the button and heard a buzzer sound inside.

"*Bonne après-midi*," a voice greeted me through an intercom.

"Good afternoon," I said. I would have replied in French but my accent is horrible, plus I felt it important to let them know I wasn't French to keep their expectations of my language skills low.

"How can we help you?" the voice, a woman's, asked in softly accented English.

"My name is Scarlett Parker and I was referred here by Ms. Harvey at the Musée du Louvre," I said. My instincts were telling me to get in the door before I admitted that I was looking for William Graham. "About acquiring insurance for an installation my cousin has been commissioned to do at a museum."

Since that was what I'd told Michelle, it was not a complete lie, at least to these people. To Michelle it had been, and now since she had been so helpful, I felt a little guilty about that, but I assured myself it was for the greater good. Right?

There was a pause and then I heard the sound of a *click* as if the door had been automatically unlocked from a remote location. Cool.

"Please come in," the voice said.

I took off my gloves and stuffed them into my pockets. Then I grabbed the cold metal handle and opened the door. I stepped into a foyer with a marble floor and one very large lone white vase, placed in the center of the space with huge plumes of feathers jutting out of it like a multicolored rainbow. It was quite eye-catching, and I wondered if I should snap a picture of it for Viv for reference. Then again, that seemed like bad form.

A petite woman in an olive green dress and killer black pumps came around the vase. She had a headset on, like she spent her days answering the phones, or I supposed in my case the door.

"Ms. Parker?" she asked. I nodded and she turned on her heel and waved for me to follow her down a narrow hallway into a series of offices.

"I'm Helena, I manage the office here. Monsieur O'Toole will be available to speak with you in a few minutes," she said. She gestured for me to go ahead into the small office and I took a seat across from a desk that was polished to such a high gloss it practically blinded me.

"Thank you," I said.

"Can I get you anything while you wait?" Helena asked.

I was pretty sure it was in her job description to get me anything I required, and for a wild moment I thought about toying with her and having her make a McDonald's run for me. But that would just be mean, so I didn't.

"No, thank you," I said. Now I wondered how this was going to go. Should I maintain the lie or come clean and hope for the best? What was the worst that could happen if I told the truth? They could toss me out on my derrière—I went with the French term as it seemed only fitting. That would be bad. Not finding Viv's husband would be worse. So, I would maintain the lie.

Minutes ticked by, well, they didn't actually tick since there was no clock in the room. I had to consult my phone to get the latest time. Repeatedly.

I debated opening an app on my phone to pass the time with a mindless game or a quick catch-up on the news, but

I didn't want to appear to be the sort of person who couldn't be still. I have no idea why this seemed important. I glanced around the room. As far as I could tell, no one was watching me, but then again, you never know, which is why I never pick anything in public . . . ever.

Aside from the gleaming desk in front of me and the soft leather chair I sat in, there was no other furniture in the room. No bookcases, vases of flowers, pictures on the walls, nothing. A glance at the window, and I saw a leafless tree outside, looking like it would crawl inside to get warm if it could just figure out how to lift its roots out of the ground. I felt a sigh start in my chest but I pinched it off. I was so close to finding Viv's husband, surely I could be patient for a few more minutes.

After what seemed like a long lunch hour but was really just twenty minutes according to my phone, a portly gentleman entered the office. He looked as fastidious as the dustless room I was sitting in. Truly, one would think that an art insurer's office would have impeccable works of art on display or at least some sort of aesthetic. This room was as barren as the grocery store bread aisle before a storm.

Monsieur O'Toole was short with chubby fingers and a bald head that was fringed with tufts of wiry gray hair. His glasses were readers and were perched on the end of his nose as if that was their permanent spot.

"Mademoiselle," he said. His accent marked him as a Brit and I was surprised to find I was homesick for the accent that I had been listening to every day for the past ten months. London really was becoming home to me. Or maybe it was just Harrison Wentworth's particular accent that I longed for, and hearing a British man, any man, made me heartsick for him. I shook my head. Now was not the time to be daydreaming about Harry.

"Welcome to O'Toole Insurance," Mr. O'Toole said. "Ms. Parker, was it?"

"Yes, Scarlett Parker," I said.

"A pleasure. Now I understand you are looking to have us insure some items for a museum," he said. He leaned back in his chair and put the tips of his fingers together as if he was holding an invisible ball.

"Yes, that's right," I said. My brain was doing loop de loops as it moved through possible segues in conversation that would get me some information on William Graham.

I could say he was my cousin—not a total lie since he was married to Viv and therefore he was a cousin of sorts. Nah, too weird. Why wouldn't I have asked for him to begin with? Of course, he was an American so I could say that I knew him from the States. Hmm, my brain churned and I was wondering if Mr. O'Toole smelled the smoke.

"What sort of items are we considering?" he asked.

"Hats," I said. I felt myself sliding down the slippery slope into out-and-out lying.

He tipped his head to the side. Obviously, I was the first to ask for that.

"I don't understand," he said. "Are these vintage? Collectible? Rare discoveries?"

"No," I said. "My cousin is a hat designer in London

and she's been commissioned to design an assortment of hats for a show featuring the fashion of, well, honestly I don't know. I'm more the people-pleasing portion of the business."

"But you're thinking you'll need the hats insured," he said. "What sort of coverage were you looking for?"

I had no clue. This is why we have Harrison as a business manager. He handles all of this minutiae for us. Why do people have insurance? I had no idea.

"Fire?" I asked. Yes, I know. I'm an idiot. It was the first thing that leapt to mind and I went with it.

Thankfully, Mr. O'Toole had a sense of humor, and after blinking at me for a moment, he busted out a belly laugh that made his middle jiggle and his double chin wag.

I smiled, mostly in relief that he had taken my stupidity as wit. Sometimes, life gives you a pass.

There was a rap on his door and Mr. O'Toole turned his attention toward it.

"Excuse me," he said. "I am expecting a report."

"Of course."

I waited in my chair while he rose out of his seat and opened the door. I glanced over his shoulder to see who I owed a thank-you to for interrupting what had become a rather stressful meeting, which happens when you have no idea what you're talking about and are busting out big fat whoppers.

My first impression was that the man on the other side of the door was impossibly tall and broad, good-looking in that straw-haired, raw-boned, "plow the field shirtless on a tractor" sort of way.

"William, just the man I was hoping to see," Mr. O'Toole said. "Come in."

The name snapped my attention to the doorway. My gaze met William's and his eyes narrowed as if he thought he knew me but he couldn't place me. Of course, I knew it was because I have the same blue eyes as his wife but how does one work that into a conversation?

"Ms. Parker, this is one of our insurance investigators, William Graham," Mr. O'Toole said. He gestured between us and William stepped farther into the room to shake my hand.

So this was Viv's husband. Huh. I liked his face. He was handsome but it was in a rugged sort of way. His features were rough-hewn, not fine, and he looked like he knew how to take a punch and, even better, knew how to throw one.

His hand was large as it wrapped around mine and his smile reached his caramel-colored eyes when he looked at me. I liked that about him, too. He had a way about him that made me think everything was going to be okay; it was a certain world-weary confidence that radiated the feeling that there wasn't much he hadn't seen, and no matter what came up, he knew how to take care of it.

Oh, yeah, it was easy to see why Viv, in mourning for Mim and feeling at a loss, fell for him so hard and so fast.

"Nice to meet you," I said. He had no idea how much!

"The pleasure is mine," he said. I gave him points for being charming as well. "But I have to say I feel as if we've met before. Could it have been back in the States, perhaps?"

"I don't think so," I said. I was very aware of Mr. O'Toole glancing between us. Now was not the moment to bring up Viv, not in front of an audience. "I have that sort of face. People always think I'm their cousin, niece, neighbor, former babysitter, you name it."

He tipped his head while he looked at me. "I'd never confuse you for my babysitter."

His crooked smile delivered the joke and again I understood why Viv had been swept off her feet. William Graham was a charmer.

"Ha ha," Mr. O'Toole laughed, making his belly jiggle. "Very good." He turned to William and said, "About that matter?"

"It was just as we suspected and it's all taken care of," he said.

"Documentation?" O'Toole asked.

"But of course," William said. "I left it with Helena."

Mr. O'Toole clapped William on the back with a hearty smack. A lesser man would have been knocked forward a pace or two, but not William. He was as immovable as a brick wall.

Mr. O'Toole glanced back at me. I could tell that he had something on his mind, so I gave him a small smile of encouragement.

"I hate to take more of your time, Ms. Parker," he said. "But I really need to pop out of the office for just a moment. Perhaps you'd like to take a tour of the offices with Mr. Graham, meet some of the staff and hear about what we do?"

He looked so hopefully at me that, even if I hadn't wanted to do the tour thing, I would have gone.

"Sure," I said. I turned to William. "If it's all right with you, of course."

"Absolutely," he said. "I'd be delighted to trot you around and show you how O'Toole Insurance operates. We're the best in the business, you know."

Mr. O'Toole beamed at him and I could see that William Graham was regarded quite highly, another point in his favor in my opinion. It struck me then that maybe the reason Viv had wanted me to talk to her first when I found her husband was that an annulment wasn't what she wanted. Maybe she wanted a reconciliation.

As Mr. O'Toole left the room, I felt as if he took all of the air out of the room with him. I couldn't believe this hadn't occurred to me before, nor had it come up in conversation with Viv. I had just assumed that if she left the man after a few weeks of being married to him, then she was done with the marriage. Maybe she had just panicked, as Viv does, and run.

"Are you all right, Ms. Parker?"

I glanced up to find William looking at me with concern. Aw, man, he was a nice guy, too. What had Viv been thinking dumping him out of the blue like that? I had no idea how I was going to manage this conversation, but I couldn't risk losing him by pretending to be a client. It was time to come clean.

"Come on, I'll give you the grand tour, including where we keep the coffeemaker and cookies," he said.

"You had me at coffee," I said. I stood up and shouldered my purse. I had unbuttoned my coat so as not to get overly warm but kept it on to fight the intermittent chill that the weather brought with it. I had noticed that most buildings in Paris, much like our apartment building, stayed a bit on the cool side. Living in London, you'd think I'd be used to the cold and wet by now, but no, I was still working on it.

He led me out of the small office and back down the hallway to a spiral staircase. It was just wide enough for two people to walk side by side and William matched his pace to mine. His legs were long enough that I suspected he usually took the steps two at a time, possibly three, but good manners had him keeping pace with me, which I thought was very conscientious of him.

Believe me, I was looking for reasons to dislike or at the very least not warm up to the man. I mean, I had to deliver the happy news that his runaway wife was in Paris at this very moment and, yeah, she wanted an annulment. It would be so much easier if the guy smelled like onions, or had nose hair that was too long, grubby fingernails, pants that were too short, or the personality of a turnip, nothing against turnips but they don't make the best of companions.

This guy, I glanced at him out of the corner of my eye, this guy was none of those things. He was dressed in charcoal slacks and a pale gray dress shirt that molded to his shoulders. He smelled faintly of almonds and spice, very manly. He was clean-shaven and his fingernails looked trimmed but not buffed. The man was not a metrosexual.

Thank goodness. I never knew what to do with a man who spent more time on his personal polish than I did.

When we reached the top of the stairs, he gestured wide at the workspace that unfolded before us. It appeared that all of the walls separating the rooms on this floor had been stripped down to make it one enormous room. There were several stations with computers, drafting tables, and other diagnostic equipment that I had no hope of identifying.

"Our first stop is the appraiser's work area, also my home base," he said.

"So, you're an appraiser?" I asked.

"I was," he said. "I was an art major with artistic ambitions but I fell into appraising and now I'm more on the investigation side of things, you know, investigating claims that are suspect, routing fraudulent art pieces being passed off as originals by authentication or attribution, truly, it's never dull."

"It sounds fascinating," I said. "This place is huge. Is there really that big of a black market for fine art?"

"Huge," he said. "There are a lot of rich people on this planet who can afford rare and beautiful things and they are willing to pay for them. Unfortunately, it takes a very good eye and a wide knowledge base to verify a work of art, and most of the people with money have neither."

"So they rely upon you," I said. "That puts you in a position of some power."

He shrugged. "I don't like to see anyone, even rich anyones, taken advantage of, but it's about more than that. For me, it's about preserving the art."

"Keeping it sacred?" I guessed.

"Exactly," he said. "And I believe you have to use all of the tools of the trade to do so."

"What sort of tools?" I asked. "I thought it was up to the experts to study the brushstrokes of a painting to determine whether it belonged to the artist or not."

"Now you're stepping into the fray," he said.

"Oh, I'm sorry, I didn't mean to offend you, Mr. Gr—" I began but he interrupted.

"Please call me Will."

"Scarlett," I said.

He looked at me for a moment and I wondered if Viv had told him about me. My name isn't that common; maybe it was stuck in his memory bank somewhere. He shook his head as if trying to get back on track.

"Sorry, I just . . . never mind." He cleared his throat and resumed lecture mode, which was not unpleasant. "What's happening in the art world now is very divisive," he said. He led me farther into the room, where I could see art history books stacked all over the place, along with microscopes and some tools that I assumed were used for taking paint samples and yet looked pretty lethal to me.

"You have the old-school connoisseurs pitted against forensic experts," he said. "Take the *Red, Black and Silver* piece by Jackson Pollock. His lover and his wife squabbled over whether it was an original Pollock all the way to the grave."

"That's some serious grudge holding," I said.

"It's what the difference between a five-figure estimate of worth and a seven-figure one will do for you. His wife hired the connoisseurs to make her case, people schooled in Pollock who knew his style probably better than he did himself, and they believed that the composition of the painting was inconsistent with his body of work.

"His lover, on the other hand, went with the forensic experts. These were people schooled in police work who also knew how to test the painting without damaging it, and they were able to find a polar bear hair in the painting that belonged to Pollock's own polar bear rug, which was on the floor of his living room in 1956, the same year the painting was said to have been done for his lover."

"Whoa," I said. "What happened?"

"That case is still at a standstill," William said. "The point being that just because a polar bear hair was found only means that the painting was done in Pollock's house but not necessarily by Pollock."

"So, they need a witness," I said.

"Yes, one other than the lover who says she got him to paint it for her after he'd taken a two-year hiatus and was battling alcoholism," Will said.

"Are all your investigations so sordid?" I asked. I could see by the gleam in his eye that he clearly loved his work.

"Only the really good ones." He laughed. "What brings you into O'Toole's, by the way? You haven't discovered an old Hopper in your grandmother's attic and want to insure it, have you?"

I glanced around the empty room. This was my moment then. I looked him straight in the eye and said, "Actually, I'm here about your wife, Vivian Tremont."

Chapter 5

If I'd zapped him with a Taser, I don't think I could have stunned him more.

He stared at me for a second and then said, "Your eyes. You have the same eyes. That's why you looked so familiar when I first saw you."

"Viv is my cousin," I said. "We own a hat shop together in London."

He stared at me like he couldn't quite believe I was standing here in front of him, talking about his wife. He turned and found a rolling chair and sat down. He leaned forward, resting his elbows on his knees with his hands loosely clasped together.

"Is she all right?"

"She's fine."

He looked at me with equal parts dread and hope, and

I felt a sudden surge of irritation at Viv for putting me in this situation. Artistic temperament or not, she really needed to curb the rash behavior. I mean, now we were wrecking marriages—even if it was her own, it was too much.

"Did she send you to find me?" he asked.

The hope in his eyes was shadowed by dread. I glanced away. It was clear to me that he was not exactly on the same page as Viv. Great, just great.

"Sort of," I said. I drew in a breath and figured this was like taking off a bandage. I could torture the poor guy by easing it off hair by hair or just rip it and get it done. "She wants an annulment."

"No!" he cried.

I glanced back at him and saw the look of alarm on his face. Great, this was going to go even worse than I had feared.

"I'm sorry," I said. "But she was very clear—"

"I don't care," he said.

That got my back up. He didn't care, eh? Those were fighting words. The look on my face must have given away my unhappiness, because he sat up and raised his hands in a conciliatory gesture.

"I didn't mean I don't care about what Vivian wants," he said. He looked pained. "I care very much about what she wants, which is why I let her go. I always thought . . . I believed . . ."

His voice trailed off and I knew without him saying it that he always believed she'd come back to him. That was a punch to the chest I could live without. His gaze when it met mine looked tortured.

"You always believed she'd come back." I said it for him.

"Yeah," he said. "Pretty stupid, right?"

"No, blindly optimistic, sure, but not stupid," I said.

He pushed out of his seat and strode over to the window. It was narrow and thick paned and looked out over the roof of the shorter building next door. He ran his finger down the inside of the glass, tracing a drop of condensation as it traveled down the outside.

"Did she meet someone else, then?" he asked.

Judging by the gruffness in his voice, the question cost him. I thought about the handsome barrister, Alistair Turner, who was pining for Viv back in London. I adored Alistair, but as far as I knew, Viv had kept him at arm's length, knowing that she wasn't available while still being married and all.

"No," I said. "There's no one."

He glanced back at me and I saw the hope flare up in his eyes again. Oh, boy, I hated to be a buzzkill but I figured it was better coming from me than Viv.

"Look, we're only here for a week, so the papers—"

"'We'?" he interrupted me. "By 'we,' do you mean you and Viv? She's here? In Paris? Right now?"

Uh-oh. I had the feeling that I might have just opened the door to more trouble. Why, oh, why didn't I ever check the peephole first?

"I . . . uh . . . it . . . we . . ." Here's a tip. Stall-stammering never helps when you're trying to avoid answering a question or five; in fact, it's a dead giveaway.

He took a few steps toward me, his gaze locked on mine. "I have to see her."

"I don't think that's—"

His rough-hewn features hardened, cementing into stubbornness right before my very eyes.

"It's nonnegotiable is what it is," he said. He crossed his arms over his chest. "If there are papers to be signed, Viv will have to meet with me, over dinner, before I agree to the dissolution of our marriage."

"But it's been almost two years," I said. "Don't you think if the two of you were going to work out, you would have found your way back to each other by now?"

"She's here now," he said. "Maybe this is us finding our way right now."

"I'll talk to her," I said. "But I can't make any promises."

He grinned and it lit up his eyes, giving him a boyish charm that was infectious. I scowled to keep myself from smiling back at him.

"It'll likely just be a quick meet-up at a café over coffee, with pens at the ready," I said. I hoped my tone was sufficiently discouraging.

He shook his head at me. "Dinner tonight."

"She'll never go for that," I said. Honestly, I had no idea if she would or not, but I figured it was best to brace him for not.

"Yes, she will," he said. He looked supremely confident.

Why exactly was that so attractive in a man? It should be annoying, but alas, it was not.

"Fine. Dinner it is, but I'm going with you," I said.

He looked amused.

"What?" I asked.

"Nothing," he said. "I've just never had a chaperone before. Somehow, I never expected to have one who was younger than me and so cute, too."

My face grew warm. I knew he was teasing me and I shouldn't feel embarrassed but I couldn't really help it if my face flamed bright pink. I could only imagine how lovely it looked with my fiery red hair.

"Flattery will get you nowhere," I said. "Where do you want to meet? That's assuming, of course, that Viv is willing to do this."

"She will. Is nine o'clock all right?" he asked.

Most restaurants didn't even serve the evening meal in Paris until after eight. We ate late in London because of the hours of the shop, but this was late even for us.

"How about eight thirty?" I countered.

"All right. Tell me where you're staying and I'll pick you up," he said.

"No, I think it best that we meet at the restaurant," I said. Just because he seemed like a nice guy didn't mean he was, and since I'd come to appreciate how valuable privacy was over the past year, I was always very cautious about my personal information such as where I was staying, etc.

He gave me a look that I was pretty sure was full of

respect as opposed to him being irritated with me, so that was nice.

"You're a tough negotiator, Scarlett," he said. "Tell you what, I'll give you my number. You can text me when you have Viv's answer about dinner and then I will text you the location of the restaurant. Does that sound all right?"

I studied him. He had an honest face, and he was clearly well liked at his job, which was a pretty cool profession for a guy brought up on a farm in Iowa. Did I trust him? Yes.

My gut instinct told me that William Graham was exactly as he appeared to be. A good guy. Still, I wondered.

"Can I ask you something?"

"Anything," he said.

"Why didn't you ever come after Viv?"

Yes, this was the one thing that bothered me. Why had he just let her walk away? He was an investigator, after all; surely he had to know where he could find his wife.

"Did Viv tell you how we met?" he asked.

"No," I said. "She's been very quiet about your marriage."

"I can see that. We met in the Jubilee Gardens in London," he said. "Well, we didn't exactly meet there, but that is where I saw her for the very first time."

"The park near the London Eye?" I asked. He nodded.

"It was a warm day in June. She was wearing an enormous red sunhat." He held his hands out by his head to demonstrate. "Her long blond curls trailed down her back over the pretty white and black dress she wore. I can still see the way it fit her curves and then flared out just above her knees. She was taking long strides in these black spike heels that made her legs look impossibly long. Pretty much every guy in the park stopped whatever he was doing to stare as she went past."

He had a faraway look in his eyes, as if the memory of that day was one that he held very dear.

"I followed her," he said. He gave me a wide-eyed look as if he was embarrassed to admit that he had done that.

"How far?" I asked.

"All the way to the Underground, where I hopped on the same train she got on," he said.

"You realize that's borderline stalker behavior," I said.

"There's nothing borderline about it," he said. "I followed her all the way to a neighborhood in London called Notting Hill, well, you know the area, I suppose."

"I do, indeed," I said. "I have to tell you that's either the most romantic thing ever, or seriously creepy."

"I know," he said. He cringed. "Even at the time, I kept telling myself I was crossing a line, but I knew if I didn't figure out where she belonged or if she belonged to anyone, I might never see her again and that was completely unacceptable."

I leaned against a steel cabinet, rested my elbow on it and then propped my chin in my hand. This was fascinating. I could not believe that Viv hadn't told me any of this.

"Go on," I said.

"On the train to Notting Hill Station, someone recognized her and called her 'Viv,'" he said. "I thought it suited her because she was exactly that—vivid and vivacious. Then she got off at Notting Hill Gate and I followed."

A slow smile spread across his face and I knew he was reliving the moment.

"I thought I was being so smart about it," he said. "But then I turned a corner, you know where you leave Pembridge Road and take a left onto Portobello?" I nodded. "Yeah, well, when I got around the bend, she jumped out at me with an umbrella in hand, a big one, and she threatened to clobber me with it if I didn't stop following her."

He laughed and I felt myself smile. He was genuinely amused at the memory.

"Honestly, with her eyes crackling blue fire and her white knuckles gripping an umbrella as big as she was, it was love at first sight," he said.

"How did you get her to put the umbrella down?" I asked.

"I was honest and told her that she looked like she had just walked out of a painting by Manet and that I couldn't not follow her at least until I knew her name," he said. "I think that is the only thing that saved my melon from a bashing."

"The art connection," I said. That made sense.

"I begged, literally begged on one knee, for her to have dinner with me," he said. "She agreed to meet me for a pint at the Duke of Wellington Pub."

"How did you go from a pint to marriage?" I asked.

"One pint turned into two, then dinner, then a walk where we never stopped talking about everything from art to music to our childhoods, then dessert, until within days we were planning our elopement and then we just did it," he said. "When she left, I thought she'd change her mind and come back, but she never did, and then . . . well, I didn't want the marriage to end, and I figured if I pushed it, she'd make it permanent, so I didn't chase her, figuring someday she'd come find me and give us another chance."

"Wow," I said.

Here I'd been holding Harrison at bay for almost a year and this guy and Viv had sealed the deal within weeks. It boggled. Still, here we were, looking to get an annulment. I couldn't forget that this was what Viv wanted now and I was in charge of making it happen.

"Yeah," he said.

"Romantic beginnings aside, Viv may not change her mind about the marriage," I said. "You have to be prepared for her to ask for an annulment tonight."

"I am," he said. "But I'm also confident that what we had was real and that if she just spends some time with me, she'll see that and change her mind."

I didn't have the heart to argue with him, plus this was Viv. I honestly had no idea how this was going to go.

"All right, then," I said. "I'll text you her decision about dinner and we'll go from there."

"Thanks, Scarlett," he said. The smile he gave me was sweetly hopeful. "No matter what happens, Viv is my wife. I will always look out for her, even if she doesn't want to give our marriage a go."

I nodded. That clinched it. As objective as I tried to be, I really liked William Graham.

Chapter 6

I managed to find my way back to our arrondissement and only went the wrong way once. The sky had cleared up, and when I walked home from the Dupleix Station, I felt the tension that had been dogging me since we arrived in Paris lift. My mission had been to find William Graham and negotiate an annulment. Now that I had met him, I sensed that things were going to work out, one way or another, and I felt as if my mission was very close to being accomplished.

As I wandered through our neighborhood, I paused to glance down the street and caught sight of the Eiffel Tower. My heart swelled just like it did whenever I saw it. I mean, seriously, it was the freaking Eiffel Tower and I was looking right at it. How incredible, rather, *incroyable*!

It struck me then that while I was fine with being here with Vivian, I really considered Paris a place for couples, not cousins. The City of Light was meant to be a backdrop for falling in love, romancing your chosen one, taking long strolls along the Seine, making vows atop the Eiffel Tower, and latching a small padlock onto the Pont des Arts Bridge—although the locks had been removed from the famous bridge a couple of years before, I still considered it a very Parisian thing.

I didn't have to think too hard to know who I would share all of this with if I had my choice. I fished my phone out of my bag and opened my contacts list. I pressed the name of the person I was missing without overthinking it. I mean, he had asked me to check in with him, so I was just doing what he'd asked. So there.

"All right, Ginger?" he answered on the second ring and just the sound of his voice warmed me from the inside out.

"Just fine, Harry," I said. "How about you? How goes saving your big investment business?"

"Who cares?" he asked. "Boring paperwork, endless meetings, dodgy solicitors, it's madness. Tell me about your quest for Viv's husband."

"I found him, actually," I said. "Making me the best cousin detective ever."

"No doubt," he agreed. "Come now, don't leave me wondering. What happened? What's he like? Is he a decent bloke or a complete git?"

"He seems . . . nice."

"Nice like porridge?"

He sounded perplexed and I laughed.

"No, not like porridge, more like a nice cup of tea," I said. "He's very good-looking, very attentive, and very polite."

"Huh." He grunted. "I think I hate him."

"Why, I'm shocked," I teased. "You sound almost jealous. He is married to Viv, remember, or is that why you're jealous?"

"Don't be daft. Of course I'm not jealous about Viv's husband. I'm jealous because you're three hundred and fifty kilometers away in the most romantic city in the world, looking at other men, married or not, and I'm here," he said. "It's a good thing I know you've got a ban on dating or I'd be mental."

I laughed. Harry was delightful. Sometimes, I found it very hard to believe that ten-year-old me had been stupid enough to stand up twelve-year-old him on our ice cream date eighteen years ago. Clearly, I had been an idiot.

Yes, this was our sordid past. We had been childhood friends and then our paths diverged until just last year. It occurred to me that Harrison might be my reward for suffering so many fools before him.

"Oh, Harry." I sighed. "I miss you."

"Would that be as your business manager or your friend?" he asked.

"As my lover, actually," I said.

There was a loud clattering noise on the other end of the line and I held the phone away from my ear as it was spectacularly loud. Did he drop the phone? The thought made me chuckle.

"Ginger? Are you there?" he asked.

"Yes, I'm here," I said. I made my voice smooth as if I didn't suspect a thing.

"Sorry, I dropped the phone," he said. His voice dropped an octave as he growled. "You are killing me, you know that, right?"

"In a good way?" I asked.

"It will be," he promised.

Suddenly the chilly day seemed overly hot and I almost shed my coat just to cool down a bit.

"Well," I said. It came out breathier than I'd intended and I heard Harry chuckle. Turnabout was fair play, I supposed. I cleared my throat. "I have to go give Viv the news that we are dining with her husband tonight, assuming she agrees, so I'll let you go."

"Call me later." It wasn't a request.

"I will."

"Bye, Ginger."

"Bye, Harry."

I walked the rest of the way back to our apartment building with a spring in my step. Only a few more months until my ban on dating was lifted. Poor Harry didn't know what was going to hit him.

Viv, Suzette and Lucas Martin were seated in the front parlor when I arrived. I had met Lucas briefly when he picked us up at the airport on the day of our arrival. He was tall and thin with a head of thick silver hair and matching eyebrows. His face was unlined, however, which made me think he had gone gray very young and was not as old as his hair would have me assume. When he smiled, it warmed his brown eyes, which crinkled in the corners, and he stood when I entered the room, always a gentleman.

"Mademoiselle Scarlett," he said. "You are looking as lovely as ever with a bloom in your cheeks and a sparkle in your eyes."

He took my hand in his and bowed elegantly over it. Lucas had charm by the bucketful.

"*Bienvenue*, Scarlett," Suzette said. "Join us for an aperitif?"

"Thank you, that would be lovely," I said. I also hoped it was a strong one since I had to break the news to Viv about our evening plans.

A tray was set on the table with several glasses, a bucket of ice, a bottle of Lillet, and a small bowl of orange slices and mint leaves. Suzette made my drink while I turned to Viv and smiled. It was not one of my better efforts.

She took one look at my face and tossed back her drink in one big swallow. She plunked the glass on the tray, looked at Suzette and said, "Hit me."

It was an expression she had picked up from me during a few of our girls' nights out at the pub. I covered her glass with my fingers to keep Suzette from complying. Drunk Viv would not do well with what was coming.

"I found him, Viv, and we're having dinner with him tonight," I said.

"No," Viv said. "No dinner. I can't. He was just supposed to agree to sign some papers. Why do we have to meet?"

"I told him that you would say no, but he is very insistent," I said.

"Perhaps I need to speak with him," Lucas said. He was scowling and I liked that he was so protective of Viv.

"That is very kind of you, but I think William needs to see Viv with his own eyes and hear her tell him that she wants an annulment." I took a long sip of my drink, which helped, and said, "I think he still wants your marriage to work."

Viv dropped her head into her hands. "Why do men always make everything so bloody difficult?" She glanced at Lucas. "Present company excepted, of course."

"Of course, *chère*," he said and toasted her with his glass.

"I need to text him your answer," I said. "You can say no but I don't think he will be as agreeable about signing the papers. You need to see him, Viv, it's the right thing to do, plus, I told him I was going with you to chaperone."

That actually made Viv laugh. "You? My chaperone?"

"What? I could be a good chaperone," I said. "I'll ask all sorts of horribly personal questions, order the most expensive thing on the menu and belch in public, really loudly. It'll be great."

Viv laughed. Then she reached over and hugged me. "What would I do without you?"

"Be bored out of your mind," I said. "Also, you'd have no clients."

She nodded. She knew that was my gift and she embraced it, which was why we were such a fabulous team.

"All right," she said. "I did prepare for this contingency, so if you'll excuse me, I am going to dress for dinner."

We watched her leave. She strode bravely from the room with her back straight and her head held high. Atta girl!

"*Mon Dieu*," Suzette said when Viv reentered the sitting room. "Viv, you cannot go out in public dressed like that. You simply cannot."

Lucas managed to keep his face completely still. The only thing that betrayed his dismay was a fit of rapid blinking that he quickly got under control.

I was speechless. In all of the years I had known Viv, which was my entire life, she had been the epitome of fashion and good taste. Yes, sometimes her hats were on the edge of the spectrum for artistic whimsy, but always she looked like she had just walked off the pages of *Vogue* or *Vanity Fair*.

At the moment, however, she was unrecognizable. In a dress the color of dirty dishwater, which swam around her figure with a sack-like inelegance, she had accessorized it with thick-heeled man boots, wool tights and a stretched-out cardigan in a puke shade of mustard.

"Where did you get those clothes?" I asked.

"I bought them," she said. "They were on sale at a thrift store in London right before we left."

"On sale at a thrift store?" I asked. "Did they even cost a pound?"

"The boots did," she said. She lifted one leg so I could get a gander of the well-worn brown leather.

Suzette, in a form-fitting heather blue sweater over black jeans, looked like she was watching a train wreck and had no idea how to stop it. She had one hand at her throat and had pressed her lips together as if to keep from saying anything she shouldn't.

"Brilliant, right?"

Viv twirled around to give us the full effect. She had scraped her hair into a knot at the back of her head and had washed her face, leaving no makeup behind. Her pretty features still shone through, but without cosmetics, they were subdued.

"I'm not really sure what you're going for," I said.

"Fashion repellant," she said. "If I dress too nicely, he'll think I want to start up again, and I definitely don't want that. But if I look like a swamp hopper, he'll wonder what he ever saw in me."

I exchanged a look with Suzette. The glance she sent me was pitying, and I knew it was because I was going to have to go out in public and be seen with Viv, like this. Oh, horror.

"Trust me," Viv said. "I know what I'm doing."

"As the only man in the room, I do believe you will achieve your goal," Lucas said.

If that wasn't an understatement, I didn't know what was. I heaved a deep sigh. This chaperoning gig was not really working out for me.

William had texted me the name and address of the

restaurant. It was far enough away that Lucas offered to give us a lift. It's always nice to have a friend with a car, isn't it?

Unlike Viv, I was not out to repel anyone, so I went upstairs to change into proper dinner attire and freshen up my hair and face. I wondered if it would bother Viv that, for possibly the first time ever, I actually looked better than she did. I needn't have worried.

"Brilliant, Scarlett," Viv said. She clasped her hands together as if she couldn't contain her excitement. "You look smashing, and in contrast I'll look even worse. William is going to sign those annulment papers so fast he'll strain his fingers."

I didn't think he was so dumb as to be bamboozled by her bad outfit, but I wisely said nothing. Instead I followed Lucas out to the car, noting that Suzette looked longingly after him as he went.

Being terminally nosy, I was curious as to their relationship. See? I know my own flaws. Nosiness is probably in the top five, okay, top two. Either way, I wondered if Suzette was pining for Lucas because he had no idea how she felt about him. Even Frenchmen, who are generally more tuned in to the female's emotional needs, are not perfect.

I maneuvered myself into the front seat with Lucas by edging Viv out at the last second. She gave me a look and I shrugged. Lucas, on the other hand, looked a bit relieved.

As we worked our way through the dark city streets, I began my interrogation.

"So, Lucas," I said. "Is there a Mrs. Lucas?"

I heard Viv gasp from the backseat. Sometimes she thinks I am too forward. She might be right but it was for the greater good.

He turned to look at me and one of his silver eyebrows lifted. "Are you asking if I am married?"

"Yes," I said. "If I'm not being too rude by asking."

"Not at all," he said. "I am not married or seeing anyone. Is there a reason why you ask?"

"No, no reason," I lied.

I glanced out the window. In France, like the States, they drive on the right side of the road. Of course, in Paris, it seemed as if they drove wherever the heck they felt like it; still, it was nice to be driving on the side of the road that I was most familiar with and I felt myself relax into the seat.

As the dark of night enfolded the city in a firm embrace, the city sparked to life all around us. I understood why they called it the City of Light; it positively glowed. It was breathtaking.

I wondered if enough time had passed for my next question, then I figured, what the heck.

"So, how long have you known Suzette?" I asked.

He glanced at me. He smiled. He looked back at the road in front of us and deftly navigated a roundabout with no signage, seriously no signage. It was like the running of the bulls but with stick shifts.

"A couple of years now," he said. "She bought that building from my brother when she was looking to start over."

"Excellent," I said. "She is a friend then, yes?"

His brow furrowed as if he'd never really thought about it before. Honestly, men are thick!

He nodded. "Yes, I would call her a friend."

"She's lovely, don't you think?" I asked. "And charming?"

"Quite," he said. The look he gave me was curious. "Scarlett, are you acting as a . . . em . . . how do you say . . . *marieur*?"

"I don't know," I said. "What is a *marieur*?"

"A person who puts together a man and wife," he said.

"A matchmaker?" I asked.

"*Oui, oui*," he said. "Quite right."

I noticed the French have a habit of saying things twice. I figured it was their enthusiasm for life and found it very endearing.

"You have figured me out," I said. I wagged my finger at him and he grinned, obviously pleased with himself. "I have a friend in London, Nick Carroll, who I think will be mad for Suzette."

Lucas stomped on the brakes and snapped his head in my direction. Horns started honking as he had not bothered to pull over.

"Lucas!" Viv cried from the backseat. "Whatever are you doing? And Scarlett, what rubbish is that? You know Nick is—"

"Busy at work?" I interrupted her. "I know but he might be able to pop over for a short holiday."

"No!" Lucas said. He stomped on the gas and we were

thrown back against our seats as he drove even more aggressively to our destination. "I do not like this idea. Not at all."

"Why not?" I asked. Of course, the whole conversation was ridiculous because Nick was gay and already shacked up with our friend Andre Eisel, but Lucas didn't know that.

"Suzette is very fragile," Lucas said. "She needs someone who can care for her appropriately."

I was silent for a moment. Then I said, "I think she is lonely."

Lucas looked stricken. Truly, how had the man not noticed that Suzette was alone in that drawing room every evening getting her companionship from a rotation of renters? I had to look away so I didn't give him my bug-eyed *Really?* look, because it's a doozy.

"Scarlett, what are you playing—" Viv asked from the backseat but I interrupted her again.

"Are you ready?" I asked. I checked my phone. I was following our progress on my map app. "We're almost there."

I was a little premature, but I knew that she'd panic and I'd better build in time for her to have a mini meltdown. Who wouldn't when they're about to see the husband they ditched over a year and a half ago? Besides that would get her thinking about her situation and not the one I was manipulating up here in the front seat. Good thing I am a fabulous multitasker, no?

"No, I'm not ready," Viv said.

"Get ready," I said. "Chez Robert is up ahead."

"I changed my mind," Viv said.

Lucas slowed to merge with traffic coming from the right. I heard the back passenger door open but I didn't register what was happening until Lucas yelled.

"Vivian! No! *Vous serez tués*!" he shouted.

Chapter 7

I looked to the back just in time to see Viv's door slam shut. Damn it! I hadn't planned on her freaking out so completely!

"Thanks for the lift," I said to Lucas and jumped out of the car after her.

I heard him shout my name as well, but I had to catch Viv before she lost me. We were only a block from the restaurant where we were to meet William in ten minutes.

I took one step forward and a tiny little car almost made a speed bump out of me. The driver honked and made a rude gesture that I really couldn't fault him for as I'd have done worse.

Viv was already on the sidewalk and I hurried after her. I had to catch her before she disappeared into the crowd.

Yes, the streets were crowded as we'd crossed over the Seine onto the Right Bank and were near one of the major tourist thoroughfares in Paris, along the Champs-Élysées.

Why couldn't William have picked a restaurant in one of the outer arrondissements, where there were less people? As if it mattered. I had a feeling either way I would be running Viv to the ground.

She was bolting down the street, and people jumped to the side to get out of her way. At least she was running toward the restaurant and not away from it, so I had that going for me. Her heavy men's boots were weighing her down, giving me an edge in the sprint-off. I caught her just before she would have turned a corner into a dark alley.

I grabbed her arm and dug in my heels. She tried to shake me off, but I was clinging like a clump of mascara on an eyelash. She was going to have to do better than this silly shimmy shake thing she had going if she wanted to be rid of me.

"Viv, stop!" I cried. "Get yourself together."

"I can't do it, Scarlett," she cried. "I can't face him."

I grabbed her by the elbows and shook her.

"Yes, you can."

"You don't understand," she said. "When I left him—"

She bit her lip and turned her head away. It was all very B movie dramatic but Viv was an artist and prone to that sort of thing, so I tried to be patient, but it was difficult. I knew the clock was ticking and Will would be waiting for us.

"What is it, Viv?" I asked. "What did you do? Did you

ghost on him and just disappear? Did you break up with him on a Post-it? What?"

She didn't answer.

"You. Are. Killing. Me." I stared at the side of her head so hard I was surprised my gaze didn't bore holes through her temple.

"We were having a lovely time on our honeymoon, very romantic, and then one night after we made love like we always did, I panicked and dumped him straight to his face," she said. "Isn't that the worst?"

I let her go and staggered back a step.

"Are you telling me that in the afterglow of newly wedded bliss, you shotgunned him?" I asked.

"When you say it like that, it sounds even worse," she said.

"That poor bastard," I said. "No wonder he wants to see you again. He's a man. If you caught him after sex, his brain probably wasn't even fully engaged before you were out the door."

"Do you see why I can't do this?" she asked.

"No," I cried. "I see why you are going to do this or I am going to kick your behind, really hard."

I lifted my leg so she could clearly see my pointy-toed shoe in the light of the streetlamp above us.

Viv heaved a sigh as if she was being tortured. I grabbed her by the arm and yanked her down the sidewalk. I was appalled. I mean, how were we supposed to stay on the moral high ground with the opposite sex when she pulled stunts like this?

I dreaded asking, but I figured I'd best be prepared. "What exactly did you say to him when you dumped him?"

She tipped her chin up in full-on defensive mode. "I told him I felt that the marriage had gone as far as it could go and I was leaving."

"And you just left?" I asked.

"Yes."

I let go of her arm but kept walking. When we had talked about her marriage before, I had assumed, wrongly apparently, that it had been because of an actual thing, like he left the toilet seat up, or the toothpaste cap off, you know, real issues for the newly married set. But no, she just freaked out and left.

"Was the sex that bad?" I asked. Truly, I couldn't think of any other reason why she'd do what she did.

"No, quite the opposite, it was lovely actually," she said. "He is very well equipped—"

"Please stop," I said. "I have to eat dinner with this man."

We continued walking. I was relieved that Viv didn't try to bolt again. But now I was confused. If the sex wasn't bad, and they were having a lovely time like Viv said, then why did she leave William? It made no sense. Of course, this was Viv—point A to point B with her was seldom in a straight line.

"If it wasn't the sex, why did you dump him?" I asked. "Because, even though I only met him for a short while, he seems like a really nice guy, and in case you haven't noticed, the planet is in short supply of those at the moment."

"I don't know." She shrugged.

"Oh, come on!" I slapped my hand against my upper thigh. Normally, I had much more patience for Viv's artistic side, but right now with an excruciatingly awkward dinner impending, I really was out of empathy.

"What do you want me to say, Scarlett?" she asked.

She stopped walking and plunked her hands on her hips. Her coat was as baggy as the rest of her outfit but at least it looked appropriate given the cold weather.

"Something that makes sense," I snapped. "Let's do a quick review, shall we? Reasons for ending a relationship include but are not limited to he's a lying cheating rat bastard, he doesn't get your motor humming, you discover he has an addiction like drinking, drugs, gambling or video games. Less on the scale of bad but still relevant would be he's a slob, he lives with his mother, he's in debt up to his top shirt button, he has poor hygiene, am I missing anything? Did Will have any of those things? Even onc?"

Viv gave me a sad look. "No."

"Then why did you leave him?"

"Because it was too good to be true," she said. "He was too good to be true. Because there weren't any of those issues you just rattled off on your breakup grocery list."

"That makes no sense," I said.

"Scarlett, love at first sight is . . . codswallop," she said. I opened my mouth to argue but she held up her hand, stopping me. "There is no such thing as a perfect man or a perfect relationship. There has to be something wrong with the person and with the two people coming together. There have to be obstacles to overcome, communication to hammer out, there need to be disappointments, arguments and churlishness, because those things lead the way to compassion, empathy and generosity. You can't have one without the other. If a relationship is perfect, there is no place for it to go."

I stared at her. Sometimes the genius that my cousin is sneaks up behind me and wallops me upside the head. She was right. There were always two sides to every coin, especially in a relationship where there are two personalities to blend.

"Just so I'm clear," I said. "You're telling me you broke up with him because it was too good and too perfect."

"Now you're catching on," she said.

"Don't you think that, given time, you might have gotten on each other's nerves?" I asked. "Maybe you just didn't give it enough time."

"I tried to be a bother, I gave it my all," she said. "But he never got upset or irritated. He just adjusted around me and whatever wild hair I had going. I knew we were doomed."

I glanced at my phone. We were near the restaurant. I looked up and checked the addresses. Sure enough, just up ahead was Chez Robert.

"Well, I guess now you'll know for sure if it really was too perfect," I said. "We're here."

Viv paled. Given that she was already pretty pasty, this washed her out even more. During our scuffle, her hair had slipped the bun she'd mashed it into and her curls fell down about her shoulders in a riot of blond loveliness. It helped soften the severity of her clothes.

I glanced at the restaurant and saw the maître d' through

the glass front door. I imagined this place usually had seating outside on the patio but the cold made it prohibitive. Too bad. I felt Viv would fare better if an escape route was at hand.

I took a deep breath and stepped toward the door. I pulled the long handle and the magical scent of good food plumed out the door to enfold us in its intoxicating lure. Okay, the drama between Viv and William aside, I was really looking forward to dining in a posh French restaurant.

Will must have alerted the staff that he was waiting for us. We were greeted warmly by the maître d', who escorted us into the dining room without pausing to ask us where we wanted to sit, if anyone was joining us, or anything.

The restaurant was all white tablecloths, candlelight and soft music. The murmur of voices and the *clink* of silverware on plates was a steady background cadence as we crossed the room behind our guide.

When we got to the far corner, it was to find William standing beside a round table tucked into the corner. He was looking very handsome in a dark blue pinstripe suit with a pewter-colored dress shirt, open at the throat.

He looked right past me at Vivian and I glanced behind me to make certain she didn't bolt out of the restaurant. Yes, I would have executed a flying tackle if I had to. Mercifully, she wasn't staging a runner, rather, when her gaze met William's, she stumbled to a halt and fidgeted with the handle of her purse.

Her mouth opened as if she would say hello, but nothing came out. She stood frozen with her big, blue eyes devouring the man in front of her as if she had been pining for him all these months apart.

Had she? I had no idea. All I knew was that the air between them positively crackled with tension, and I was pretty sure it was the good sexy kind and not the bad "they are about to choke each other out" kind.

"Viv, you look . . . beautiful," he said.

I could tell he meant it, despite her best efforts at being frumpy. Viv blushed a bright pink, making her even lovelier.

Still, she didn't speak and William turned to me, although it looked as though he had to force himself to do it, and said, "Scarlett, you look lovely as well."

"Thanks," I said. "Viv?"

She hadn't moved and other diners were beginning to stare. Slowly, as if she had to remind herself of how it was done, she put one foot in front of the other.

The maître d' pulled out a chair for me, while Will did the same for Viv. She stared up at him as she took her seat and I could see the doubt on her face. I knew without asking that she was wondering if she had done the right thing when she left him. Well, we had all of dinner to figure it out.

Chapter 8

"Gretna Green," I said. "Really? I thought that was just some made-up fluff out of a Jane Austen novel."

"Oh, no, since the mid-eighteenth century, when the age for marriage was changed to twenty-one, couples have been hopping the border into Scotland to tie the knot. Back then, the Scots only required a person to be sixteen and to have two witnesses, much easier back in the day," Viv said. "And dreadfully romantic."

"So, it really is an elopement spot and you two ran off there?" I asked. I knew it and yet it still stunned me, although why, I don't know—this was Viv after all.

We were two bottles of wine and several courses into our meal. The wine combined with fine French cuisine had mellowed us all considerably, and Will finally broke down and, with a nod from Viv, told me the finer details of their elopement.

"Yes, we did," he said. He lifted his hand as if he would put it on top of Viv's where it rested on the table, but he clearly thought better of it and snatched up his fork instead.

We had already enjoyed grilled scallops with celery saffron sauce, white asparagus with dried pomegranate, and now we were working our way through tarragon-spiced salmon on a bed of mushroom and spinach risotto. It was amazing, and I was so glad we were savoring each course as it gave us plenty of time to deal with the ginormous elephant in the room, namely, that two of our threesome were married, and as yet, I had no idea what they were going to do about it.

"Do you remember driving up there in the middle of the night?" William asked Viv.

"Of course," she said. She ducked her head. She actually looked shy. Then she laughed. "We left London at midnight and drove the five and a half hours straight through, except for that dodgy loo stop in Manchester."

William burst out laughing. "You came tearing out of the bathroom, screaming because you were sure that someone had tried to break in."

"It wasn't funny," Viv scolded but her blue eyes were twinkling when she turned to me. "It was a rat, a big one."

Behind her back, William was holding his thumb and index finger up where I could see, indicating that the "rat" was about the size of a kiwi. I snorted. Viv whipped around and saw him and lightly slapped his shoulder.

"Oh, you," she said.

It was the first time she had touched him and they stared at each other with an awareness that was impossible to miss. Feeling very much like a third wheel, I figured I should probably excuse myself and go for a nice walk around the block in the bitter cold. Oh, joy.

My self-sacrifice was stalled when William's pocket started to chirp. He pulled his phone out of his jacket pocket and silenced the ringer. He looked at the display and frowned. He was obviously not eager to speak to whoever was calling.

He glanced at us with regret. "I am so sorry; I must take this."

"Of course," Viv said.

I nodded.

He rose from his seat and took his phone out to the lobby. I watched as he put the phone to his ear. He was pacing by the front door, back and forth. He was too far away and his voice was too low for me to pick out any words, but it was apparent that he was not happy, as in, super unhappy.

Viv was watching him, too, but the look on her face was vastly different than my speculative gaze. She watched him with eyes that sparkled, lips that were parted, and with a flush on her skin that screamed she was a woman in love. Oh, sweet chili dogs! Now we had a situation.

"Viv," I said her name. She didn't respond. "Viv."

Still nothing. How could she be oblivious to me, her cousin?

"Hello, in there." I waved a hand in front of her face. "Anyone home?"

Viv waved me away with a frown. She met my gaze and the dewy, puppy love expressions were gone, replaced by one that was more normal for Viv in regards to me, irritation.

"What is it?"

"Are you still in love with him?" I asked.

"What?" she cried. "How can you ask such a thing?"

The waiter, who was very attentive but not at all as forward as David from the bistro in our neighborhood, pity, interrupted what I was about to say as he cleared away our last course and brought another. It was a cheese plate and it was beautiful.

Our waiter explained that these were cheeses from a local *fromagerie* and identified them as Brie de Meaux, Coulommiers, Merle Rouge and Brie Noir, which is an aged Brie with a black crumbly rind. Also on the plates were several small loaves of freshly baked bread and an assortment of berries and jam.

As soon as he left, I helped myself to some cheese and bread. It was a fortification for the conversation ahead. I swear.

"Viv, when you look at him, you look like you want to run away with him all over again."

"I don't," she said.

There was a hesitation in her voice. I knew I didn't need to point it out because she pressed a hand to her chest as if she heard it herself.

"Really, I don't," she said. "It's just . . ."

Her voice trailed off and I knew it was time to remind her of why we were here. First, I took another nibble of cheese. Smooth and creamy, with its soft-ripened rind, I was in heaven, so it was very hard to focus on the task at hand. I took a sip of wine.

"What happened to your leaving him because everything was too easy, too perfect, that there was no balance to the relationship, no struggle?"

"I said that?" she asked.

"Less than an hour ago," I said.

"Huh, fancy that," she said.

Her gaze darted past me to the man in the lobby. I turned around just in time to see William pocket his phone, but instead of coming back to our table, he pushed out the door.

"Is he leaving?" I asked Viv.

"So it would seem," she said. She frowned.

I watched him walk outside to the corner. I wasn't even trying to be subtle about it. I craned my neck and leaned halfway across the table.

The couple at the table near us exchanged a glance but I didn't care. I wanted to know what Will was doing. Would he really leave us? Was this his revenge for Viv ditching him? Take us out to a nice restaurant and then stick us with the bill? I wondered if I should chase him down.

I'd lost more dignity over lesser situations. I glanced back at the cheese plate. I really didn't want to leave it behind.

"Is he meeting someone else?" Viv cried.

My head snapped up. Now that would be even worse than sticking us with the bill. I craned my neck again to get a gander out the window.

Sure enough, a car and driver pulled up to the curb outside the restaurant. This was no mean feat in one of the busiest streets in the neighborhood. I watched as the tinted window in the back rolled down.

Will stood with his arms crossed over his chest and frowned at the passenger. If the person in the car was trying to intimidate William, it wasn't working. His cheeks were ruddy, either from the cold or his temper, it was hard to tell, but he looked very forbidding in that moment.

"Oh, my," Viv sighed.

Obviously, I was not the only one who noticed.

"Well, at least your husband hasn't run out to meet another woman," I said. The angle of the streetlight overhead cut into the car just enough for me to see the sleeve of a man's suit coat.

Will made an impatient gesture and I tried to read his lips. I suspected they were speaking in French because I couldn't decipher a word of it. It was easy to read the body language, though. William was furious.

"There's that," Viv said. "What do you suppose is the issue?"

"Well, he is in the insurance game as an investigator," I said. "Maybe he has an unhappy client."

As if aware that he was the subject of our scrutiny, Will turned back to the window and caught us blatantly watching what was happening. In our defense, he did leave the restaurant without telling us what was happening. Isn't it natural that we should want to see what had become of him?

He seemed to get that. With his back to the car, he

opened his eyes wide and made a gesture like he'd like to strangle the person in the car. Viv snorted.

"I forgot how funny he is," she said. She waved at him and he smiled before making his features stern and turning back to the car.

"So, should I get used to thinking of him as my cousin-in-law?" I asked. "Oh, man, what are you going to say to your parents?"

No, Viv's mom and dad, who lived up in Yorkshire, had no idea that she'd tied the knot. Do you see how frustrating she can be? Even her parents didn't know about Will. I swear it's like living with someone who works for MI-5. I gave her a side eye. Could she possibly . . . Would that explain . . . Nah, that'd be ridiculous, right?

"I'm not going to say anything," she said. "I mean, I've only been reacquainted with him for an hour. I have no idea how this is going to work out."

"So is an annulment off the table?" I asked.

"Nothing is off the table," she said.

I took a sip of my wine. "Well, as far as I'm concerned, the case of the missing husband is solved. What happens now is up to the two of you."

"Do you think—I mean, I know he said he wanted to give the marriage a go but do you think he meant it?" Viv asked.

She looked vulnerable, and I glanced out the window to see Will turn on his heel away from the car and stride back toward the restaurant. He had seemed sincere when I tracked him down at his office but did I know him well enough to determine whether he really meant it or if it was just a whim? No, I didn't. Still, Viv looked so fragile, I wasn't up to crushing her when I knew she had so much going on inside of her right now.

"He seemed very sincere when we talked," I said. "And he seems to be trying to put his best face on." I gestured to the table and the restaurant around us.

"He does have a nice face," she said.

"I hope you're talking about me and not the waiter," Will said as he rejoined us at the table.

Viv looked flustered but I laughed. William really did have an easy charm about him, which was so good for Viv as she tended to get caught up in her creative fevers and forgot to eat, or sleep, or laugh.

"I apologize for leaving you during the meal," he said. "I received a call from a client, and when I told him I was at dinner, he informed me that he was just down the street. I figured it was best to meet him directly."

"Forgive me for being rude," I said, "but I'm going to be anyway."

Viv gave me a look but I ignored her.

Will nodded for me to continue while he sliced off a bit of the fresh bread and helped himself to the cheese.

"You did not seem to be happy to be talking to the man in the car," I said.

"I wasn't," he agreed. "He is a very powerful art buyer, and he thinks that by threatening me, he can get whatever he wants. I disagree."

"What does he want?" Viv asked.

Her eyes were wide and she looked at him in alarm. I could understand it. She had just found him; it probably didn't make her feel easy to know that someone was threatening him.

"If you two aren't in a hurry to get home after dinner, I'd like to show you something," he said.

We both nodded. Curiosity clearly runs in the family.

Chapter 9

It was a romantic walk, albeit freezing, down the famed Avenue des Champs-Élysées. I was sorry that we had missed the Christmas lights that illuminated the famous street during the holiday season, but it was still festive and full of activity as we strolled past the exclusive shops, restaurants and nightclubs. The sidewalk was full of tourists, and occasionally I had to dodge to the left or the right as Will and Viv were too involved in each other to notice the pedestrians around us.

He had taken Viv's hand and put it on his arm and they put their heads together in a whispered conversation as we walked. I couldn't hear what was being said over the city noises around us, so I was left to follow like an uninvited guest.

It occurred to me that I should have had Viv change

outfits with me before we left the restaurant, because clearly I was the dowdy dowager in this threesome. I was trying not to let it pound my self-esteem into the dirt. It was a struggle.

Although my lay of the land for Paris is a bit sketchy, I knew we were moving away from the Arc de Triomphe and back in the direction of the Musée du Louvre, which was where Will's office was located. I wondered if he lived in the vicinity as well. I opened my mouth to ask him, but saw that he and Viv were too busy staring into each other's eyes to give me their proper attention. Fine.

I heaved a sigh and trudged on, trying not to get distracted by the shops, Louis Vuitton and L'Institut Guerlain being particular weaknesses for me. I mean, handbags and perfume, what's not to love?

Just as my dogs were beginning to bark—I hadn't really worn shoes appropriate for strolling—William turned back and waved me forward.

"Viv looks chilled," he said. "I'm having a car pick us up. Is that all right with you?"

I wanted to throw myself at him and hug him in relief; instead I gave him a small smile and a shrug.

"Sure," I said. I supposed I should just be glad that they didn't ditch me, since that was clearly their modus operandi. Okay, that was mean, but I was cold and tired and very, very single.

The car that arrived within minutes was large and spacious. The driver was in a suit. Classy. He held the door open and Viv gestured for me to go first. I gave her a quick look. I knew she was arranging the seating so that she would end up next to Will. All right, then, I figured I had better get her alone so I could ask her if she wanted me to leave the two of them to figure things out on their own.

Clearly, this had gone beyond a "just signing annulment papers" situation. I wondered what Harrison would make of all this and I realized I missed him terribly and not just because I was in the most romantic city in the world, dateless, but because I really valued his input on everything that was happening, and over the telephone was just not cutting it for me.

The warmth of the car enfolded me like a hug. I slid all the way across the bench seat in the back and Viv climbed in after me.

"Do you want me to go?" I asked in a half whisper.

"Go where?" Viv asked.

"You know, away," I said. "To leave you two alone."

Viv looked startled and then Will climbed into the car, preventing her from answering. She did, however, shake her head at me so I took that as a no.

A part of me was dreading the drive to William's office. I mean, being stuck with two lovebirds in a car could make anyone want to fly the coop, but it seemed both Viv and Will were aware of the awkwardness of my situation as they neither held hands nor whispered together in that annoying way couples have when they're besotted with each other. I made a promise right then and there that if, no when, Harrison and I were a couple, I would not be that annoying.

"This class that you are teaching at the Paris School of Art," Will said to Viv, "when is it over?"

"The last class is on Friday, and then we have a fashion show on Saturday where my students will show off their creations." She looked wistful. "Scarlett and I will go back to London on Sunday."

William nodded. Then he grinned. "So, what you're saying is I have some time to change your mind."

Viv opened her mouth to protest but he shook his head and she closed her mouth.

"Let's just see what happens, all right?" he asked.

I was trying not to watch their interaction; okay, that's a total lie. I was leaning on Viv, trying to gauge her reaction to his words. To my surprise, she simply nodded.

Okay, then, this was going to be an interesting week. Was Will going to romance Viv back into his life? What about Viv's complaint that the relationship had all been too easy with no struggle, no counterpoint to the good? Was that just her crazy artistic temperament ruining a perfectly good thing or was her point valid? Now that she had caused strife between them, did they have the balance she had been looking for?

That made me think about my relationship with Harrison. Was it too easy? Was it effortless with no struggle?

Ah, no, he and I tussled quite a bit, mostly about my inability not to mind my own business but also he had no appreciation for my very punny way with language.

Then, of course, there was my issue with his owning the controlling interest in our business. That one was on Viv and her weakness for Swarovski crystals, when she had let Harrison bail her out of debt without telling me, before I came back to London to take up my share of the shop.

Harry and I had obstacles, not huge ones and certainly no trust issues, just more of the "cap on, seat down" stuff, which I thought added spice to the whole trying to love someone in spite of his inability to decorate his apartment or maintain any food in his refrigerator.

I was pulled out of my reverie as the car drew to a stop in front of William's building. The driver held the door open for us and Will instructed him to wait as we wouldn't be very long.

"*Oui, Monsieur*," the driver said with a nod.

Instead of going in the front door as I had that morning, Will led us to a side door that I hadn't noticed before.

At my questioning glance, he said, "Staff only."

The door opened into a coatroom. Several lonely jackets and one umbrella hung on pegs along the wall. William paused to punch in a code and then we moved through another door into what appeared to be a staff lounge.

"This is very high security for an insurance agency," Viv said. "I'm impressed."

Will looked at her and his straw-colored hair flopped over his forehead. "Oh, my dear, this is nothing."

We followed him down a hallway. It was dark and I noticed he didn't switch on the lights as we went, which I thought was odd but then figured he probably knew his way around here and didn't think about it too much.

A narrow door at the end of the hall had a scanner beside it. As I watched, Will scanned his entire hand. After a moment the light on top of the scanner turned green and I heard the sound of a lock click.

Will glanced at us over his shoulder and wagged his eyebrows at us. "This is all very hush-hush."

Viv and I exchanged a glance. I noticed we both stood up straighter as if taking this more seriously now.

Will pushed the door open and led the way into the room. It was a plush waiting room with a large table in the center and a couple of armchairs off to the side. I was relieved that he switched on the overhead light as the track lighting around the room didn't really illuminate the space.

At the far end of the room was a huge vault door just like the sort you'd see in a bank. William gestured to the two plush armchairs off to the side.

"Wait here, if you don't mind," he said.

Viv and I sat down. The chairs were squashy and comfortable although the room was very chilly. We watched silently as he opened the vault and disappeared inside.

"Do you know what he's doing?" I asked.

Viv shrugged. "I can't imagine what he wants to show us. Can you?"

I shook my head. I thought back to our conversation earlier in the day about his work and how it was his job to investigate claims for both pieces that went missing and to prove the provenance of others. I wondered if he'd been tasked with researching something like the Hope Diamond. That made my heart pound in my chest for, while I liked art and all, a big dazzling sparkler was really more my jam.

"Here we are," Will said. He was carrying a large wooden crate, the sort used to box and ship paintings. He laid it on the wide table and Viv and I rose from our seats to join him.

The wooden top wasn't fastened, so William simply pried it off with his fingers and set it aside. Inside in a nest of cardboard, bubble wrap and brown paper was a small painting about one foot high and two feet wide.

To me it looked old and very dreary with a predominantly green cast to it and, frankly, it was boring. A landscape. Blch.

Viv, on the other hand, staggered back a bit. She gasped and covered her mouth with her hand as if it was, well, the Hope Diamond or something equally impressive.

"Is that . . . could it be?" she cried.

William beamed at her. They really were a match made in heaven if they both found that painting so exciting.

"I remember studying this piece in art school. I thought it was lost," she said. "Wherever did you find it? It is authentic, isn't it?"

"I think so," he said. "Of course, we need to bring in an expert on it, but we are fairly certain and the initial forensic testing holds up."

"Okay, I give," I said. "Why is the drab little painting so exciting?"

Viv gave me a disappointed look. "With all the time that Mim dragged us to museums, you can't recognize a Renoir when you see it?"

"Oh, is that the artist?" I asked.

"Really, Scarlett," Viv huffed.

"Art major." I pointed to her then I pointed to myself. "Hospitality major. There is a difference."

"Still it's a Renoir," Viv said. As if this should make a difference to me. It did not.

I shrugged. I saw William glancing between us and figured it was a good time to get this discussion back on track.

"So, what's the story here?" I asked. "How did you come across this painting?"

William clapped his hands together. He looked delighted to be asked.

"This piece was bought with a box of throwaway books that a junk shop owner bought at one of the *bouquinistes* along the Seine for twenty euros," he said. "Can you believe it?"

"You mean someone bought this from one of the book stalls?" I asked. I loved the *bouquinistes*. They were a Paris treasure, and one of the reasons that the Seine was called the only river in the world that runs through two bookshelves.

Viv goggled at him and then she slapped his arm. "Stop it. You're teasing us."

"I'm serious," he said. "And it gets even better. The junkshop owner then sold the painting for ten euros to a woman who just happened to stop in his shop."

Viv yelped. "Ah! I can't stand it."

"What's it worth?" I asked.

"If authenticated, this painting could be worth several million," William said.

"That's crazy," I said. "But wait, how did you get it?"

"The woman who bought it suspected it might have value, so she brought it to us to appraise and insure if need be, but, and here's where it gets whacky, O'Toole Insurance already insured this painting for the museum it was bequeathed to over sixty years ago."

I blinked at him. "But if the museum lost it or it was stolen, then O'Toole probably already paid it out so O'Toole owns the painting?"

"If it is indeed the original painting," he said. "I have to do some research, but if it is the painting that Estelle Brouillard bequeathed to the Musée de l'Or, who then insured it with O'Toole Insurance, then it has been missing for a very long time."

"That is incredible," Viv said.

"And now you know why that man, Emile St. James, was harassing me," he said. "He's an art collector who wants this painting very badly for his personal collection."

"Would O'Toole sell it to him?" I asked.

William shrugged. "It has to be authenticated first."

"How?" Viv asked. "Do you have an expert on Renoir who can verify it?"

"We're flying one in," he said. "But I also have to provide a paper trail, showing that O'Toole did actually pay the insurance claim to the Musée de l'Or when the painting was reported missing in nineteen seventy-four."

"Do you have the records for that?" I asked.

"Yes, in musty old file cabinets in our storage facility," he said.

He looked delighted while I couldn't think of anything

I'd rather do less. I'm a people person and paperwork really isn't my thing.

"You could always ask the museum to turn over their financials for that time period," I said. "Wouldn't it show a deposit from the insurance payout?"

"Yeah, shockingly, they don't really want to help me with this and instead want the painting back," he said.

"That's a bloody mess then, isn't it?" Viv asked.

"Even worse, the junkshop owner wants the painting back as does the woman who bought it from him and brought it to us. I'm just waiting for the owner of the *bouquiniste* to weigh in, too," he said. He glanced back at the piece. "Just think, this landscape has been missing for decades. We're the first ones to see it in forever."

Viv was duly awed. I was less so. Now don't mistake me, I thought it was totally cool, I just wasn't as ga-ga over art as the two of them, firmly establishing my place as the third wheel.

"*Arretez!*" a voice shouted from the door. "*Arretez!*"

Chapter 10

"Yah!" I shrieked and jumped.

"*C'est bon*, Frederick," Will said. He held up one hand at the security guard who charged into the room. "*C'est moi.*"

I sagged against the tabletop and noticed that Viv did as well. My heart was hammering so hard in my chest, I missed most of the conversation between Will and the guard. It was clear, however, that the guard was unhappy at finding the three of us in the vault room.

William moved to stand beside the guard and his voice dropped an octave. He gestured back at Viv and I saw the guard glance around William to check her out. I did not need to translate the French they were speaking in my head. It was quite clear that William was explaining to the man that he was trying to make time with the blond babe.

"*Oui, oui*," the guard said. He bobbed his head and gave a chuckle. Obviously, guy commiseration for picking up chicks was a universal condition.

I glanced at Viv and caught her watching Will. She looked impressed by him and I wondered if it was the painting, his knowledge of the painting or his ability to speak French.

I felt the need to play devil's advocate. Shocker, I know.

I leaned close and said, "I'm pretty sure Alistair Turner can speak French, and probably German, too."

She turned to look at me on a slow roll that I knew gave her time to think about her answer before our gazes actually met.

"I'm married to Will," she said.

"For now," I said.

Yes, I was needling her. Back home in London, I knew our friend Alistair waited to see what the outcome was of this adventure. He was a rugby mate of Harrison's and spectacularly good-looking with chin-length dark hair and a wicked smile. He was also an excellent attorney, which we knew firsthand as he had helped Harrison out of a jam recently, not to mention another of our clients when she was wrongly jailed for murder.

Alistair had been very direct about his interest in Viv, and Fiona Felton, our intern at the hat shop, and I had been mystified by Viv's reaction and her ability to keep him at arm's length. Of course, now I understood why but at the time it had boggled.

Viv gave me a quelling look as Will joined us. I liked Will, I did, and if the marriage between them worked out, that was great, but I didn't want Viv to forget that she had options. Plus, she had left him for a reason, whether I understood it completely or not.

The security guard left us with a smile and a wave. Will began to repackage the painting. He took great care with it and I thought that spoke well of him.

I had dated men who didn't take care of their things, and I always thought it was indicative of how they would treat their relationships. I'm not talking about being super fussy or annoyingly fastidious, just conscientious. If a man treats his things poorly, like not taking the time to change the oil in his car regularly or letting his refrigerator get funky, then it's likely he won't want to put in the time to maintain his relationships either, leaving all of the heavy lifting and maintenance to his partner. Who needs a man like that?

Viv and I waited while he returned the painting to the vault. She didn't say anything and I didn't press it. I was sure she must have a lot on her mind and it wouldn't help if I pestered her about everything.

"Thank you for humoring me," William said. He closed up the vault behind us. "Since the courts decided that we could hold the painting here until its ownership is determined, I've been dying to show it off to someone. I'm so glad it was you."

He was talking to Viv, not me. The air got thick and I knew when it was time to exit stage left.

"I'll just wait for you two out—"

They charged each other and were already lip locked before I finished my sentence. I turned on my heel and headed out to the hallway, where all good chaperones cooled their heels while their wards made out, or snogged, as Viv would say.

The hallway was quiet and dark. There was no sign of the security guard. I took out my phone and noted that it was later than I thought. I wondered if Suzette would wait up for us. If it was me, I would, but then, I do have that nosiness issue.

I debated texting Harry but then changed my mind. I didn't want to explain that Viv was making out with her husband, because Harry was best mates with Alistair and I didn't want him to feel weird about the whole thing. Oh, no, I was going to keep the weirdness all to myself. Yay, me.

Instead, I decided to text my best pals, Andre Eisel and Nick Carroll. They were my first friends in Notting Hill when I returned to London and we'd been through quite a lot ever since that first meeting. Andre was a photographer who ran a studio down the street from our hat shop while his partner, Nick, was a dentist. I knew if anyone would appreciate my dilemma, it was them.

Help. I've been tossed into a hallway while Viv smooches her husband.

I knew that they might be out and miss my text so I tried to think of what else I could do while I waited for Viv. My phone chimed and I glanced down to see the screen lighting up.

Our Viv can be rather mouthy. That was from Nick. I smiled.

I hope she tells him how she really feels and isn't just giving him lip service. And that was from Andre. My smile widened.

The punsters were in full gag mode, and judging by the string of emojis after each text, they were having a grand time. I felt the need to join in the fun, which for the record never goes well for me.

I'm sure it's on the tip of her tongue, I texted back and heard crickets, as in nothing. I texted again. Oh, come on, that was a good one.

Still nothing. Then a picture came through and it was a selfie picture of Nick and Andre giving me dead bored stares. Ha! I knew they were just giving me a hard time, and it made me laugh and miss them terribly.

Idiots. XOXO, I texted back.

Just then the door opened and a very flustered Viv stepped out with Will right behind her. They both looked a wee bit disheveled and they were grinning like fools. On the one hand, I was happy for Viv, but on the other hand, it sure made me miss Harry.

"Sorry about that, we were—" Will started to apologize but I waved it off.

"It's fine," I said. "I know you have stuff . . ."

This time my voice trailed off in embarrassment. They exchanged an amused glance and Will took Viv's hand in his and led the way down the dark hallway, leaving me to follow. I stifled a sigh, barely.

"I'm sorry I can't escort you all the way home," Will said. "The pressure is on for me to authenticate that piece so I'm afraid I'll have to work into the night."

"It's fine," Viv said.

Personally, since things had gotten hot and heavy between them, I figured it was just as well that they separate for a little while so Viv could get her sea legs.

We stepped back out into the cold, and I pulled on my gloves and tightened the scarf about my throat. William closed the door behind us, and as we left through the side exit, I saw the guard through the window standing in the front office drinking a mug of coffee or maybe tea.

The night air was turning bitter so we didn't linger but hurried back into the car that was parked and waiting for us. The driver saw us coming and hopped out of the car to open the door for us.

I climbed in and then I heard Will tell the driver that he'd get the door. At least that's what I think he said because the driver said, "*Oui, Monsieur,*" and went back to his driver's seat while Viv and Will loitered outside the car.

I exchanged an embarrassed look in the rearview mirror with the driver. The car was warm but the open door was making it drafty and it was all I could do not to encourage Viv to get her derrière, see, I was picking up the language, into the car.

I debated pulling out my phone again but resisted. Mostly, because I was sure they wouldn't linger over their good-bye in the cold. I was wrong. There was the distinct sound of smooching and I saw the driver smile.

"*L'amour jeune,*" he said. I knew enough French to know he said, "Young love."

I nodded but in my head I was thinking Viv was a little

old to be playing the young love card and so was Will. I glanced at the driver. He had gray at his temples and his face was lined and it seemed more from worry than laughter. That made me feel bad for him. I wondered if he'd always been a driver for a living or if his backstory had more to it.

I would never know. While I debated our driver's life story, the sound of screeching tires drew my attention, and I glanced up to see a sleek black vehicle, much like the one Emile St. James had been in earlier that evening, come careening around the corner.

I heard Will swear, and when I glanced out of the car, he was taking Viv's arms from around his neck and pushing her into the car.

"*Allez! Rapidement!*" he snapped at our driver. The other car stopped near ours and Will stepped back and shut the door.

"Will!" Viv cried. That was all she got out as our driver threw the car into reverse, trying to back away from the car that was blocking us.

Viv and I stared out the window, watching as two men in dark clothes approached Will. He immediately put his fists up in a fighter's stance.

"Stop!" Viv cried. She reached forward and slapped the driver on the shoulder. "*Arretez!*"

The driver shot her a look as if he thought she might hit him again, then he shoved the car into drive and stomped on the gas.

"No!" Viv cried.

She turned and pressed herself against the window. I

did, too. We were just in time to see the two men jump Will, subdue him, and toss him into the back of the car before it drove off.

Our driver, clearly terrified, took off in the other direction, taking rapid turns at a breakneck pace, which flung Viv and me across the backseat like a couple of rag dolls.

"Stop!" Viv shouted. "That is my husband. We must follow that car. We must stop them."

The driver gave her a look like she was crazy, but he did pull over and stop the car. In thickly accented English, he said, "Get out!"

Chapter 11

"Do you have William's number?" Viv asked. Her voice was amazingly calm, given that we'd just been dumped on an obscure side street and her husband had been abducted.

"Yes," I said. He had texted me about the restaurant. I turned on my phone and showed it to her. She didn't hesitate but punched the number into her phone and began to pace while she waited for him to pick up.

"It's going straight to voice mail," she said.

"That means he's either using it, its battery is dead or it's shut off," I said.

Viv left a quick message to call her and then ended the call.

It was cold and dark and the street seemed ominously quiet. I glanced around, hoping to see a Metro sign in sight.

There was nothing. Our driver had ditched us in a neighborhood in Paris I had never seen before.

"I can't believe that driver just abandoned us," Viv said. "I'm going to report him."

"Not really our biggest problem right now," I said. "What's the emergency number in France?"

I had my phone out and I was trying to remember what number to call. I had no idea.

"One-one-two, same as back home." Viv had her phone in hand as well and began to tap in the numbers.

"I thought it was nine-nine-nine in the UK," I said.

"It is. It's also one-one-two, which is what most European countries use," she said. "Oh, hello, yes, an English speaker, please."

While Viv proceeded to describe what had just happened to the emergency dispatcher on the phone, I decided to call Harrison. He was our business manager; he would want to know what was happening to us. Okay, yeah, and I just wanted to hear his voice so I could calm down.

"Hello, Ginger," he answered on the second ring.

"Harry, thank goodness," I said. I tried to keep my voice even, but hearing his voice made my emotions rise up, giving my voice the wobbles.

"What is it?" he asked. "What's wrong? Are you all right? Are you safe?"

"We're fine," I said at the same time that Viv said the same thing to the dispatcher.

She gave me a look and I said, "Harry." She nodded and returned her attention back to her phone.

"What's happening, Ginger?"

Quickly, I told him about Will taking us to dinner and showing us the painting at his office and then how when we left the office, Will was abducted and our driver dumped us on the side of the road in Paris and that Viv was on the phone with the Paris Police at the moment.

"I'm calling a cab to come and pick you up," he said. "Have Viv tell the police to meet you at your apartment building."

"But—" I began but he interrupted me.

"No buts," he said. "Tell her."

I tugged on Viv's sleeve and told her what he said. She nodded. She looked relieved that someone had a plan.

"Okay, I told her," I said.

"Good," he said. "Now tell me where you are exactly."

I glanced at the corner. It was a whacky intersection with five roads all converging and there was no signage. I studied the buildings all around me and noticed that there was a café behind me, closed for the night, but maybe the name would be enough of a landmark.

"I know we're in the fourth arrondissement," I said. "We're standing in front of a place called La Vie de Café."

"Perfect," he said. "I'll send someone for you. Do not move."

"Thanks, Harry," I said.

"Call me if anything alarms you for any reason," he said.

"I will," I said.

I ended the call and glanced at Viv. She was fretting her lower lip between her teeth and staring out into the night as if she could conjure Will out of the darkness.

"What did the police say?" I asked.

"They seem quite unconcerned," she said. "They kept asking me if I was sure Will was abducted or if he might have willingly gotten into the other car. I don't think they believed me. Still, they're going to send someone around to our apartment to talk to us."

"Harrison said he was sending a car to collect us," I said.

"Thank goodness for him," she said. I wholeheartedly agreed.

"What do you think happened?" I asked. "Do you think it was Emile St. James, the collector who pulled him out of dinner to talk about the painting, maybe he won't take no for an answer?"

"I don't know," she said. She reached out and grabbed my hand. "I'm frightened for him, Scarlett."

"I know," I said. I squeezed her hand hard and then let go so I could wrap an arm about her. She looked scared and cold and lonely, and I didn't know what to say or do to make it any better. I kissed her head and then I lied, because that's what you do in situations like this, and said, "It's going to be okay. We'll find him. I promise."

Suzette opened the door to us with a big smile, looking eager to hear about Viv's reunion with her husband. The looks on our faces must have alerted her to how horribly awry the night had gone because she reached out and grabbed our hands and pulled us into the drawing room.

"Oh, *chères*," she said. "What is it? What happened?"

"Will," Viv said. Her voice sounded small and fragile. "He was taken, abducted right in front of us."

Suzette looked at me and I nodded. "It's true. Have the police been here?"

"No," she said. She glanced between Viv and me, looking worried. "Come in and have a brandy, it will settle your nerves."

Sounded like a plan to me. We followed her into the drawing room, where a fire was crackling and the room was mercifully empty of other guests.

There was a decanter of Calvados on a tray with several small glasses. She poured one and handed it to Viv. I noticed Viv's fingers were shaking when she took the glass. Suzette handed me one as well. I didn't take a drink but was grateful to have something to do with my hands.

"Sit, sit," Suzette insisted.

It was nice to have someone telling us what to do. The cab driver that Harrison had sent to pick us up arrived swiftly but spoke no English, so it was a fretful ride through Paris as we wondered what had happened to William and what we should do about it.

Viv took a bracing sip of the brandy and then told Suzette everything that happened. She told her about the painting and how William had walked us out, about how the big dark car arrived and Will had looked prepared to fight but they snatched him instead. Then she told her how the driver had abandoned us and that when Viv called the police, they didn't feel as if there was much to go on, so they said to go home and they would send someone to talk to us.

Suzette listened with her eyes wide and a hand to her throat as if she just couldn't believe that such a thing had happened.

"I don't know what to say," she said. "I am so sorry that your husband was taken, but what a brave man, to push you into the car and insist that the driver take you away from the danger. I am so very glad the two of you were not harmed. The world is a terrifying place sometimes."

I knew she was referring to the terrorist attacks that had happened in Paris in the recent years. Random violence, hatred, culture clashes, power struggles, it changed things whether we all acknowledged it or not.

Viv and I took off our coats and settled in to wait for the police. Suzette stayed with us, leaving only to go and make a cheese plate for us to snack on while we waited. I was too full from our amazing dinner to be hungry, but I was so anxious from what happened, I found myself comfort eating a thick slice of Brie on a crusty piece of French bread.

Even Viv picked at a few of the small grapes on the plate. She rose from her seat to pace a few times and checked her phone once or twice as she had given the police dispatcher her number. We debated calling again, but it seemed pointless since they hadn't been very encouraging the first time we called.

As my adrenaline ebbed and the Calvados and cheese worked their magic on me, I found myself dozing on the couch. I was worried about Will but I was also exhausted. Feeling powerless to do anything to help him, exhaustion was winning the battle for my consciousness and I felt my head bobble on my neck a few times before I gave up and let it rest on the back of my seat. I was just going to close my eyes for a second, I promised myself.

The buzzer from the foyer sounded and I snapped upright. It took me a second to get oriented, and when I did, I noticed that Viv and Suzette were doing the same. We all must have sacked out. The buzzer sounded again and Suzette jumped up to answer it.

"Wait here," she said.

"It's probably the police," I said to Viv. I rubbed the sleep out of my eyes and glanced at the clock on the wall. We'd been back at the apartment building for two hours. "Not that I think they can help. In all of the chaos, I never got a look at the men who grabbed Will. I don't know the make and model of the car or the license plate."

"Me either," Viv said. She sounded despondent.

We sat waiting for several minutes. I was just about to go and see what the holdup was when I heard Suzette and a man, speaking in rapid French. My heart banged up into my throat. I knew that voice.

Harrison Wentworth strode into the room, and I was pretty sure my heart was going to explode out of my chest.

"Harry!" I cried. It wasn't a fully formed thought. It was pure instinct. I jumped up from my seat and ran across the room and threw myself into his arms.

Chapter 12

"All right, Ginger?"

He didn't even rock back from the impact. He just folded me into him, hugging me tight, and for the first time I realized how truly frightened I'd been by the whole encounter. The familiar bay rum and citrus scent of him was infinitely reassuring, as was the steadying look in his bright green eyes.

I stepped back from him even though it was the last thing I wanted to do, and moved aside so that Viv could have a hug as well. I knew she likely needed it more than I did, but it was still very difficult to share.

Suzette was watching us and I explained, "This is Harrison Wentworth, our business manager."

She nodded. "He said as much, but I was worried that perhaps he was one of the abductors."

Oh, sure, there was a part of me that would be more than happy to be abducted by Harrison. I thought it spoke well of me that I didn't say as much.

"We'll get it sorted, Viv, I promise," Harrison said. He was holding her by her upper arms and staring intently into her face. She looked confident for the first time all evening.

I knew exactly how she felt. With Harrison here, it seemed as if everything would be all right. Speaking of which, I had to ask.

"How did you get here so fast?"

"Company jet," he said. "We were planning to liquidate it as an asset but I am really glad we held on to it for a bit. I'd have been mental if I was stuck cooling my heels in an airport in the middle of the night trying to get here, and it's a six-hour drive so that wasn't feasible either."

I smiled. If our positions were reversed, I knew I would feel the exact same way.

The buzzer on the front door sounded again and Suzette went to answer it. This time it actually was the police, which was excellent timing because now we could tell Harrison and the police at the same time and not have to repeat ourselves.

The man who came into the room was young, in his early thirties was my guess. He had thick wavy dark hair, a prominent nose, which looked to have been broken once or twice, and full lips. He smelled faintly of tobacco and coffee and wore a heavy overcoat over his suit. He showed his badge to Suzette and then Harrison before fully entering the room.

Introductions were made, and the man identified himself as Inspecteur Lavigne. Harrison took over the conversation from there with input from Suzette.

I didn't know about Viv but I felt comforted having a frontline like Harry and Suzette to navigate our talk with the police. I didn't want him to dismiss what had happened because we were clearly visitors and had almost no information to give him.

Harrison spoke to the policeman in French just as he had with Suzette. Until tonight, I had never heard him speak in another language, and I have to say it was pretty hot. Not that this was the time to be having thoughts like that, but hey, I was exhausted and this was Harry, my Harry, and he was here and he was speaking French like a native. Honestly, a girl can only take so much.

"Vivian, can you tell Inspecteur Lavigne what happened?" Harry asked.

I glanced at Viv and she nodded. The motion caused her blond curls to bounce around her shoulders and I noticed Lavigne appreciated the gesture.

We all moved to the couch and chairs and sat down. Suzette and Lavigne took the chairs while Harry, Viv and I took the couch. The inspector listened intently while Viv described the events of the evening. His face was impassive and I couldn't guess what he was thinking. When she finished, he was silent for a moment and then he frowned.

"I am sorry, *Madame*, but I must ask," he said. "Do you know of anyone who wanted to harm your husband?"

His voice was thick and rich and very soothing. I was betting he was a very good policeman as I've noticed over the years that the best police are the ones who know how to talk kindly to people. Since most police only deal with people in times of dire distress, I always thought it spoke well of the ones who could be kind and patient, instead of abrupt.

"My husband and I have been apart for some time," Viv said. "I am afraid I don't really know who is in his life presently, other than that man he spoke to at dinner."

"Emile St. James?" Inspecteur Lavigne clarified.

Viv nodded.

"His place of employment is O'Toole Insurance," I said. "I met his boss, Monsieur O'Toole. He may have a better idea of who in Will's life might be holding a grudge. He investigates claims for high-priced art. There might be someone who is unhappy with him."

Inspecteur Lavigne nodded. He glanced between us. "Is there anything else?"

Viv and I exchanged a look. I couldn't think of anything. She shook her head. Neither could she.

"I'm sorry," I said. "That's all we know."

He nodded. "I will contact his employer first thing in the morning." He pulled a thick white business card out of his coat pocket and handed it to Viv. "If you think of something or if you hear from him, please call."

"I will," she promised.

We all stood and Harrison walked Inspecteur Lavigne out. Once they were out the door, Viv slumped back onto the couch. Her blues eyes were filled with worry and tears. I sat beside her and squeezed her hand.

I didn't bother to speak because I knew that saying it

will be okay only works so many times, plus the visit with the inspector had made the situation much more real.

"What if it's a kidnapping?" Viv asked. "They won't call me. No one even knows we're married. Will they call his parents back in Iowa? How will I explain who I am to them?"

"Easy," I said. "We don't know what's happening yet. Tomorrow, I will go to the insurance office and talk to Mr. O'Toole and see what he can tell me about what Will was working on; maybe there was a problem with a different claim."

"I'll go with you," Viv said.

"No, you need to teach your class," I said. "Your students paid an awful lot of money to attend and it wouldn't be fair to them for you to skip out. Besides, we have no idea what this is about yet. Maybe it was nothing."

Viv looked at me and I knew from the look on her face that she didn't believe that this was nothing. Far from it. I didn't believe that either but I also didn't think she was the best one to go around asking questions. As we all knew, dealing with people was not her gift, it was mine.

"You'll stay in touch with me the entire time?" she asked. "And you'll take Harrison with you."

"Yes to the first, absolutely, but I don't know about the second," I said. "He may have to get back to London."

"Viv is right," Suzette said. "You should have an escort if you are going to ask questions about Will's disappearance. It could be dangerous."

"Which is why I am here," Harrison said as he reentered the room. "And I'm not leaving."

I suppose it was totally inappropriate that my heart did a little tap dance of joy that Harry was here in Paris with me. I glanced at Viv, who still looked shell shocked and miserable. Yes, it was wrong of me, I got that, and yet, I just couldn't help it. Me and Harry, solving a missing person's case in Paris together. Totally romantic, right?

The sleeping arrangements were my first indicator that this was going to be more problematic than I had anticipated. All of Suzette's apartments were occupied, which left Harry sleeping on the couch in our living room. Thankfully, the sofa was long enough to fit him, well, if he squinched up a little bit, but still, Harry was asleep mere feet away from me.

Have I mentioned that I've been celibate for almost a year now? Mostly, because I was busy hating all men, it hadn't been a problem, but this was Harry. Other than my two gay friends, Andre and Nick, he was the only man, besides my dad, who had managed to worm his way into my inner circle of people I liked and trusted.

It was more than just physical attraction with me and Harry, although there was a truckload of that, it was also that I just flat out adored him as a person. He was funny and kind, patient, and had a self-deprecating humor that always made me smile. He was also a heck of a kisser. What can I say? There had been a couple of circumstances where kissing had been impossible to avoid. Really, absolutely unavoidable.

And now he was sleeping on the other side of a flimsy door, you know, those things that swing on hinges, making it so easy to actually open and close them and sneak into places you had no right to be in the middle of the night. Yeah, those things.

This was not good, really not good, as a test of my self-control. I am the person who will circle the refrigerator, wherein lies the last piece of cake, for an hour convincing myself that if I just take a nibble, no one will notice until predictably there is nothing left on the sad little plate but some crumbs and a pitiful dab of frosting, which I will invariably swipe up with a finger.

Yeah, me and self-control are not boon companions; in fact, I don't even let it ride shotgun with me. So, having six-feet-plus of Harry separated from me by a lousy door, really, there needed to be a dragon in between us, a fire breather at that, if I was planning to still be celibate upon our return from Paris.

I tossed. I turned. I thrashed. The night was fitful, as all the romance novels say. During the many times I woke up, I wondered if Harry was sleeping any better than I was. Then I wondered what exactly I thought I'd do with him since Viv was on the other side of the apartment separated by just as flimsy a door as ours.

Yeah, that nipped and tucked the dilemma. With Viv so close and suffering the worst sort of confusion, lost the husband, found the husband, then lost the husband again, I would never shack up with Harry right in front of her. It would be insensitive at best and heartless at worst.

Still, the close quarters were a game changer and I knew

there was only one person who could absolve me of my present dilemma, my mom.

It was early evening in Briar Creek, Connecticut, the small town where my parents had recently moved so my father could ease his scientist self into semiretirement while still working part-time at Yale. I took a chance that my mom would be home and would answer her phone.

"Hello, pet," she answered. Her soft British accent wrapped around me like a hug. "Is everything all right? Isn't it about two o'clock in the morning your time?"

"It is," I said. I dragged the comforter off my bed and wrapped it around me so I could huddle in the farthest corner of the room from the door. It wouldn't do to wake anyone up with this conversation. "Honestly, I'm having some trouble sleeping."

"Is something bothering you? Can I help?"

"More like someone and, yes, in fact, you can," I said. Now here is where I needed to segue into my pitch to be free of my one-year vow. My mother loved me. Heck, I was her only child. Surely, she would see her way to relieving me of this horrible burden of celibacy.

"I know I agreed to not date anyone for a year," I said. "But—"

"Aren't you supposed to be in Paris, helping Viv with her hat-making class?" she interrupted as only a mum can.

"Yes, we're in Paris," I said. We hadn't told her that we were looking for Viv's husband, because Viv's mother is my mother's sister and I didn't want to put my mother in the position of having to lie to her sister, so yeah, I was lying to my mother instead. Awesome.

"Scarlett, you aren't getting your head turned by a charming Frenchman, are you?" my mother asked. She sounded unhappy. "When you have that nice Harrison waiting for you in London."

So, this was good. She was looking out for Harry. They had met when my parents came to visit the previous November and I knew that both my parents liked him. Maybe this wasn't going to be so hard after all.

"Actually," I said. "Harry's here."

"Here? Here, where?"

"Here in Paris, with us," I said.

"Oh," she said.

It was a loaded "Oh." You know, the sort that carried a hint of understanding, a dash of sympathy, and a dollop of disappointment.

"Scarlett," she sighed.

"He had to come over for business, so now we're here together in the most romantic city in the world," I said. "Mum, I am not made of stone."

"No, you're not." She laughed, long and loud. I would have been offended if I hadn't been trying to press my case.

"So, what I'm wondering is—" I began but she interrupted me.

"Is whether I will let you off the hook on your vow not to date for a year?" she asked.

"Yes." I squeezed my eyes tight and clenched my fist in the comforter.

"Oh, dearest, of course I will," she said.

"You will?"

"Absolutely," she said. "I just want you to be happy." I

felt myself relax in relief. "Besides, it will be so wonderful being able to tear the Mickey out of you for the rest of your life."

"What?" I squawked. It came out very loud and I immediately lowered my voice before commencing my whine. "But Muuuuuum."

Her only response was to laugh. By "tear the Mickey out" of me, she meant that she would tease me unmercifully if I gave in on my vow now. She was a heartless woman. I told her as much and she laughed even harder.

Giving up, I told her I loved her but not as much as Dad and then I promised to call them both when we got back from Paris, oh, and I was quite sure I'd still be single and it was all her fault.

She told me she loved me, too, and hung up, still laughing.

See? Heartless. Cranky, I dove back into my bed and proceeded to sulk. It is one of my more refined skills. After a while, pouting got boring and I couldn't help but think that I was lucky to be able to pout over my man, who was here, unlike Viv, whose man was MIA. With my perspectacles firmly in place, it was pretty easy to let it go and resign myself to waiting out the next two months, alone.

Remembering the purpose of our trip to Paris helped lull me into a deep sleep and I managed to get a few solid hours in before Viv was once again in my bedroom, commanding me to wake up.

"Scarlett, wake up." She jostled me. I burrowed deeper. "Scarlett, I have to go. Mr. Martin is waiting."

She wasn't going to go away. I pulled my covers down and sat up. Harrison chose that moment to appear in the doorway.

"Good morning," he said. He looked cheerful and then bewildered. "What is on your pajamas?"

I glanced down. Oh, hell's bells. I was wearing my rubber duck pajamas. If there was an ejector button on my bed that would send me flying out of the room, I would have hit it hard.

"Nothing," I said and pulled up my covers at the same time that Viv said, "Rubber ducks."

"Well, I guess they really fit the bill," Harry joked.

Viv snorted. "I call fowl on that one."

This time Harrison hooted, and said, "Thanks, I was just winging it."

My eyes rolled back into my head. I had a feeling this could go on all day.

"You two are really quacking me up," I said. They both looked at me with perfectly blank faces. I was outraged. "No, no, no, that was a good one. Admit it."

My cousin and friends were quite the punsters, and ever since I had arrived in London, they had quipped and barbed one another, but whenever I joined in, they never laughed. I am quite certain it was a joke among the lot of them to tease me and they were relentless.

"Don't get your feathers all ruffled," Viv said.

Harrison chuckled and added, "Indeed, no need to be down in the mouth."

"That's it!" I cried as the two of them stood there smiling. "I am getting dressed so shoo. We need to go look for a missing husband, in case you have forgotten, so quit goofing around."

I regretted my words as soon as they flew out of my mouth. Why, oh why, didn't we have a real-life rewind button? So much stupidity could be avoided if we just had a second to rethink it.

Viv's face fell and she turned away from my bed with a shaky nod. "You're right. I'm sorry."

She spun on her heel and fled. I gave Harrison a beseeching look and he nodded. "I'll go after her and make sure she's okay."

"Thanks," I said. I felt like a complete heel. I hadn't meant to be so harsh. Right then and there, I promised myself I'd make it up to her. I would find William Graham no matter what.

Chapter 13

By the time I had pulled myself together and joined Harry and Suzette for what remained of breakfast, Viv was long gone. After I carb loaded with some *viennoiserie* pastries and washed them down with hot coffee, Harry caught me up to speed as we hit the streets.

He had already called O'Toole Insurance, posing as a client, and talked to Mr. O'Toole, who told him that Will was not in the office today due to unforeseen circumstances.

We assumed that Inspecteur Lavigne would be stopping by O'Toole Insurance, so we opted not to pursue it further . . . for now.

Instead, we decided to follow the only other lead we had.

"Do you really think we'll just find him at home?" I asked Harrison as we trudged down the narrow neighborhood street where William Graham lived.

My spirits had been in the dumper after my bout with foot-in-mouth disease with Viv, so I had donned a raspberry beret in an effort to cheer myself up. Yes, it was a nod to Prince the musician and to Paris, and even though it clashed horrifically with my fiery red hair, it did pick up my mood and it kept my head warm, so that was something.

"No, although that would be nice," he said. "But I think it might give us some ideas of where to look for him."

"How?"

"We can talk to his neighbors and see what they know about him," Harrison said. "Maybe the people who grabbed him stopped by his home first. Maybe someone saw them."

"How did you get his home address?" I asked. "He's not listed and I didn't get the feeling that Mr. O'Toole would be the sort to share his employee's information without the proper legal documentation."

"I called Alistair," he said. "He used some of his legal connections in France to finagle the address out of O'Toole Insurance."

"Alistair who is smitten with our Viv?" I asked.

"That's the one," he said. "I figured he had a vested interest in finding Viv's husband."

"And it wasn't awkward?" I asked.

"Alistair is a smart bloke," Harrison said. "He knows that the only way to win Viv's affection is to clear up the situation with her husband. Also, he likes Viv enough that if staying with her husband is what she chooses, he will gracefully bow out."

"Gracefully, huh?" I asked. I'm not really sure what made me do it. It was like the devil flew into me, and I turned to look at him and asked, "Would you be graceful about it?"

He stopped walking. The air around us remained frosty but the sun shone brightly today and I could feel its heat on the side of my face. Then again, maybe that was Harry's stare, intense and direct and hot, hot, hot.

"No," he said. Then he turned and continued walking.

Wow, just wow. How did one surly "no" make all of my girl parts sigh in the most ridiculously besotted way? It just did. I hurried after Harry.

You know how when things are really good, so good that you just can't help but push for more? Yeah, that was me. I couldn't be content with a sexy, gravelly response that rocked my world. No, no, I had to push.

I was panting when I caught up to him and fell into step beside him.

"So, when you say 'no,' you mean—" I began but he interrupted.

"No."

"'No' as in you wouldn't be graceful, or 'no' as in we're not talking about this?"

"The latter," he said.

Of course, this just caused me to press him further.

"Why not?" I asked.

He spun toward me then. I turned to meet him, hoping for what, I do not know. That's a lie, I was hoping he'd kiss me. There, I admitted it. Our faces were just inches apart; he totally could have but he didn't.

Instead, he narrowed his eyes at me in a look that devoured. *Oh, my!* Then he took a step forward. Instinct had me stepping backward. He took another and so did I until the white stone building behind me was at my back and there was nowhere to go.

He raised his hands on the wall, one beside each of my shoulders, caging me in. His face was as serious as a heart attack.

"Ginger, I am spending my nights on a sofa just mere feet from where you are sleeping, with a flimsy door in between us. I would say I'm sleeping, but there is no sleep happening given the situation, which I am trying to be very respectful about—"

"But you—" I was about to tell him he didn't have to be. Damn the consequences, which would be hearing my mother gloat for the rest of my natural-born days and all that, but he interrupted.

"No." He held up his hand. "If we start talking about us, I am going to kiss you, if I kiss you at this point, it won't be enough, and you'll end up breaking your vow of celibacy."

"You think you're that good of a kisser?" I asked. Yes, I was taunting.

He didn't say a word, he just looked at my mouth with wicked ideas sparkling in his treacherous green eyes, and I felt my face fire hot like a beacon.

He grinned. I frowned. We were most definitely at an impasse on this topic and I was pretty sure he'd just made his point. Was this the strife Viv had been talking about? It kind of made sense now, you know, in that whole "nothing worth having is worth getting easily" sort of way.

"Fine," I said, which of course meant it wasn't.

In a conciliatory gesture, he grabbed my hand in his and pulled me along the uneven sidewalk.

"If it makes you feel any better," he said, "if you had an ex pop up in your life at this point in our whatever this is, I'd likely punch him right in the mouth and then abscond with you and make you mine."

My heart took the express elevator down to my feet, and I felt dizzy at the rush. Did he really just say that? It was macho and ridiculous and I loved every scrap of it.

I leaned close and put my lips near his ear, and whispered, "And I'd let you."

He closed his eyes for a moment and blew out a breath. Then he shook himself from his head to his feet, like a dog in the rain.

"Come on, Ginger, before this conversation makes me rethink all of my good intentions," he said.

I let him lead, which right there let's you know how rattled I was. Again, I wondered if there was a loophole in the promise I had made my mother. Darn it.

We took a couple of sharp turns through even narrower streets in the neighborhood. Finally, we matched the building number to the one Alistair had given Harry. He'd said that William's apartment was on the third floor.

I glanced up at the red brick building. The third floor was the top one. On the first floor was a cigar shop with the words *Tabac Noir* scrawled in cursive on the awning that hung over the main door. The pungent aroma of tobacco grew stronger as we approached.

"I am going to stop in the shop and see if anyone knows or has seen William," he said. "Wait here and keep an eye on the door."

"Will do." I nodded. The door that led upstairs to the apartments was just to the right of the shop. It had a glass window, which I peeked through to see a small vestibule.

I waited until Harry went inside and then I made my way over to the door. It seemed to me I should at least try it to see if it was locked. It wasn't, so I stepped into the vestibule. It was a narrow space with white tile floors and a line of mailboxes built into the wall. Since no one was in there, I decided to try the interior door. It was locked.

I pondered my options. I could go back out and wait for Harry. I could wait until someone came down—

The interior door opened and I put my head down and grabbed it, holding it open for the young woman who came striding out talking on her phone. She barely glanced at me, so I stepped into the building, letting the door swing shut behind me.

Now if people are going to just open doors for you, shouldn't you take advantage of the opportunity and continue on your way? I thought so, too, so I began to jog up the first sets of stairs. Thankfully, I have to climb two sets of stairs at home every day and I was hardly winded by the time I got to the third floor, which was also the top.

I had to shake out my legs a bit before I could stride down the hallway, looking for William's apartment. It occurred to me as I went that I didn't know which one was his. They were numbered 7, 8 and 9. The doors were shut and there were no name plaques beside the doors. Darn it.

I felt my phone vibrate in my purse and I answered it as I walked back to the staircase.

"Hel—"

"Where are you?"

"Inside the apartment building," I said. "I'm on the third floor, which number is William's?"

"Meet me in the lobby, now," Harry barked.

He was mad. I didn't see why. Since he refused to give me the number, I was the one who had to walk back down and then back up again. I had walked all day yesterday. Even with all of the seasonal snacking I had done over the holidays, I really did not need this much of a post-holiday workout.

I trudged back down the steps. I could see Harry waiting in the vestibule through the door's glass window. He looked peeved. I shrugged at him and he looked even more annoyed. So much for that. I opened the door and he strode in.

"What were you thinking?" he asked.

"Someone came out and I went it," I said. "There really wasn't much to think about."

"Clearly," he said.

"Not nice," I said.

"Well, pardon me if having you disappear brings out the surly in me," he said. "I'm so sorry I care."

His hair was sticking up on his head as if he'd been running his fingers through it and there was a bit of frantic in the set of his mouth as if he'd been pressing his lips together to keep from screaming. Poor guy.

I rose up on my toes and kissed his cheek. "You're right. That was thoughtless of me. I'm sorry."

His shoulders dropped and he reached out and pulled me in for a solid rib cracker of a hug.

"It's all right," he said. "Just don't scare me like that again, please."

I'd actually just been apologizing to get him over his irritation with me, but now that I saw how freaked out he'd been, I actually meant it.

"I promise."

"Thank you."

"But why are you so rattled? What did you find out?" I asked.

"Quite a bit, actually. The man working at the counter at the cigar shop told me that some very dodgy-looking men were here yesterday, looking for William."

"Really?" I asked. "Did he know why?"

"No, he just said they made him nervous so he hustled them out of the shop as fast as he could," Harry said. "He told them that he hadn't seen William in days, which he told me was, in fact, true."

"We should go check upstairs," I said.

Harry nodded.

By the time we reached the top, the burn in my thighs made me want to weep. I refused to let it show, however, shaking my legs out as Harry walked ahead down the narrow hallway to the apartment on the end. Of course it was on the end. I should have guessed.

The other two doors were quiet. I didn't hear any music

or television noise, and I wondered if everyone was out for the day. Or maybe they were all dead. The thought made the pit of my stomach clench, repeatedly. Yeah, because I had to go there, to the darkest place possible.

Harrison reached out to knock on William's door. I grabbed his arm at the last second, stopping him.

"Wha—"

"Shh," I whispered. "What if the bad guys are in there? What if they've taken over the whole building? What if it's like a zombie apocalypse or something?"

Harrison frowned at me then he snorted.

"I'm not kidding," I insisted. "I heard a story on the news last year, or the year before, there was a zombie event in Scottsdale, Arizona, and this zombie bride was actually found dead in a casket."

"That's mental," Harrison said. "Who could even think of such a thing?"

"I'm just saying that crazy things can happen," I said. "And maybe something crazy happened here. I mean, don't you find it creepy that there's no one about?"

"It's midmorning on a Tuesday," he said. "I'm sure they're just at work. These flats don't come cheap, you know."

"Still, be careful," I said. "There's a very creepy vibe here."

He gave me an exasperated look and then raised his fist and rapped on the door. There was no answer. He waited a moment and then knocked again, louder. Nothing. I gestured to myself and he nodded.

"Will," I cried at the door. "It's Scarlett, are you all right?"

There was no answer. Harrison and I exchanged a look.

"Maybe he's out," I said.

Harrison reached for the doorknob. I fully expected it to be locked, thus ending our search, but it wasn't.

Chapter 14

"Stand back," Harrison said.

Curbing the urge to argue, I moved behind him. He turned the knob and pushed the door open. I glanced around his shoulder and gasped.

William's apartment looked as if a bomb had gone off. Furniture was overturned, papers were strewn all about. Pillows had been knifed and their innards yanked out.

"We should call the police," he said.

"Yeah," I agreed. "But shouldn't we go in and check that William isn't here unconscious from a head injury or something?"

"Good thinking," he said. "You stay here."

"No." I shook my head.

"I had to try."

"It was a good effort."

"Stay beside me and do not touch anything."

"Promise," I said.

It was a small, one-bedroom apartment with just the bare necessities. When I looked more closely at the clutter, the papers were just newspapers and magazines and the furniture was the minimum. There was no sense that a person actually lived here. There weren't any dirty dishes, no pictures on the walls, no jackets or scarves tossed across the back of a chair. Then again, maybe I was just a sloppy housekeeper.

No injured body was found in the main living room–kitchen area, so we moved to the bedroom. Harrison went in first, and I followed. The same lack of personality filled this room, too, but it looked as if someone had been here making a mess. The sheets on the bed had been tossed. A stack of books on the nightstand had been dumped on the floor.

"I'm going to check the loo, just in case," Harrison said.

I nodded. I'd let him have that one. I had no desire to find my cousin's husband dead in the tub or worse.

Instead, I went over and looked at the books. I thought it might give me some insight into the man who was William Graham. A mystery novel, very promising, a cookbook, fascinating, and a book on Renoir, not surprising given the painting I knew he was trying to authenticate.

I didn't pick the books up but left them on the floor so the police would see the room exactly as it had been left. It hurt my heart a little bit to let them just sit there on the hardwood floor but I shook it off.

Across the room the dresser had been gutted. Drawers

hung out haphazardly and clothes had been yanked free and tossed about the room or left to hang sloppily from the open drawers like a tongue hanging out of an open mouth.

The top of the dresser was bare and I glanced on the floor to see if whatever had been on top had been swept clear. I got the feeling that whoever had searched this place had been angry.

I felt a crunch under my feet and glanced down to see the back of a picture frame. I knew I wasn't supposed to touch anything but this was the first personal item I had found in the whole apartment and I was pretty sure I would actually die from curiosity if I didn't look. Not an exaggeration, I swear.

I hunkered down, and since I was still wearing my gloves, I gently flipped the frame over. It took me a second to see through the cracked glass to the photo behind it, and when I did, my breath caught.

"Nothing in the loo," Harrison said from behind me.

I didn't answer. I was too caught up in the photo. It was a close-up of Viv and William, obviously on their wedding day. Viv in a lavender-colored dress, with her blond curls swept to the side, was wearing a felt saucer hat in a shade of deep purple. It was trimmed with matching silk and organza flowers and several curled quills. It was definitely one of her finest creations. William was beside her in a dark suit with a white dress shirt and a tie in the exact same shade of purple as Viv's hat.

That wasn't what made my heart squinch up in my chest, however. No, it was the look on Viv's face as she gazed up at Will that cracked my heart wide open. Her lips were parted in a smile as bright as the sun, her eyes merry as they took on the dark hue of her hat. William was gazing down at her in an amused fascination as if he couldn't believe she was actually there by his side.

"Oh," Harry said as he gazed over my shoulder at the photo.

I could feel his weight at my back and it steadied me. I didn't know how I was going to tell Viv what we had discovered. I didn't know what it meant. And now, I didn't know what to think about her relationship with her husband.

Before, I had thought it was just another one of her crazy larks, but this, this photo, it was evidence that at some point, Viv had been very much in love with William Graham. It made my throat get tight.

"I wonder if I should take the picture with me," I said. "To give to Viv, you know, as something to remember him by."

"Steady, Ginger," Harry said. "It's not as if we've found him dead or anything."

I glanced over my shoulder at him. "But we have no idea where he is or who has him or why."

"Which is why we need to wait and proceed with caution," Harry said. "I'm going to call Inspecteur Lavigne and then I think we need to visit Viv at the art school and let her know what's happening."

I nodded. I flipped the picture back over, feeling guilty as I did so, as if I wasn't doing enough to find Will.

Harrison and I left the apartment just as we'd found it, shutting the door behind us as we went. Inspecteur Lavigne sent two uniformed officers to the apartment building. Harrison did the talking since the conversation was in French, and I tried to look innocent and charming, instead of guilt-ridden and miserable, which was what I felt.

The officers said that Inspecteur Lavigne would be in touch and that we were free to go. We didn't hesitate but quickly departed, hurrying for the Metro that would take us to Viv.

The Paris School of Art was housed in an old factory building on the Left Bank or La Rive Gauche, as the French would say. The building was made of white bricks and stood several stories high on the end of a narrow street overlooking the winding river below.

It had been many things, a factory, a storage facility, and a youth hostel, before it became the Paris School of Art, but the new occupation seemed to suit it as it had plenty of light from the north and sat in the heart of an area so many struggling artists had once called home, like Picasso and Matisse, even writers like Hemingway had resided in this neighborhood.

The sense of history swirling around me as I walked down the street made my mind wander as it always does. So much life and death had been fought for in these streets. So many centuries of struggle, triumph, shame and grandeur had been endured in this place that it made my own existence seem very fleeting.

That thought made me rethink the conversation with my mother. Did I really care if she teased me for the rest of my life? Well, yeah, I did. But what if something happened to me or Harrison like it had with Vivian and Will? What if he got snatched and I never saw him again? Could I bear it, especially if I wasted the time we could have been together, proving a silly point, that I was okay on my own, to my mother? I didn't think I could.

"All right, Ginger?" Harry asked.

We stopped in front of the massive wooden door that led into the courtyard of the school. It was on the tip of my tongue to tell him what I was thinking but I didn't. Now wasn't the time. Instead, I just nodded.

"Yeah, I'm good," I said.

He looked dubious but he didn't press it. Instead, he pulled open the oversized door and gestured for me to go first. Viv had told me that the courtyard was where the factory workers used to take lunch. It had been remodeled since then and there were wrought iron chairs, potted trees and a couple of fountains, dry for the winter, scattered all around the big space.

The main office was tucked just inside a door on the right. I glanced through the glass window and saw Lucas Martin talking to a woman with steel gray hair who was seated at a desk in the main room. I assumed she was his administrative assistant.

I waved and Lucas waved back with a smile. In a few moments, he stepped outside, shrugging on his coat as he joined us.

"Scarlett, Harrison, good to see you," he said. The men had met earlier that morning when I was still rising and Harrison was trying to smooth over my harsh words to

Viv. Lucas's expression was wary and I realized that he probably assumed we were coming with news.

"Afternoon," Harrison said as they shook hands.

"Hi," I said. "We don't have any information, at least nothing about William's whereabouts."

Lucas frowned. "That is unfortunate. I know Viv was hoping to hear something today."

"Can you direct us to her classroom?" I asked. "I'd like to check in with her myself."

"Of course," he said. "It will be my pleasure to escort you."

Honestly, the French just have a way about them, don't they? It's like suave is in their DNA or maybe their drinking water, then again, perhaps it was the wine.

The building housed two floors of classrooms and Viv's was tucked into the far corner of the building on the second floor. We crossed the courtyard and went up an outside staircase that led to a balcony above. We walked down to the end, where I could hear Viv's voice as she directed her students in the making of their hats.

Much as I lacked any skill in hat making, I knew the schedule of creation. Viv had given the students the choice of three different styles to make. All required being shaped on a wooden hat form. While those dried, they were to design how they wanted to trim the hat. The goal was to have a fashion show on Saturday night at the same time that the rest of the art classes would be having their shows.

"Excellent," Viv said. "Now when you're designing the embellishments for your hat, you want to make sure it matches the tone of the event you're planning your hat for, for example, if it's a wedding, you don't want too much sparkle or bling as it would be bad form to compete with the bride."

Lucas gave us a faint smile and stepped back. "Please let me know if you need anything else."

Harrison and I nodded. For one second, I debated bolting. If we ran away right now, Viv would never know we'd been here. That seemed preferable to telling her that William's apartment had been ransacked, we had no idea where he was, oh, and he kept a picture of their wedding day on his dresser.

Harrison was braver than I. He rapped lightly on the door as a warning and then he entered Viv's classroom. I followed, trying not to think about how less stressful running away would be.

Viv glanced at us as we entered her classroom. Her face looked wary as if she was afraid of bad news. Harrison shook his head, letting her know we hadn't found him. Her shoulders slumped and I really wanted to go over and hug her but the room full of strangers gave me pause.

There were three large tables with six students at each. Materials were strewn all over the tabletops, and I saw the students riffling through the ribbons and beads and silk flowers, as if they were Dumpster diving for their last meal.

"Excuse me," Viv said to her students. She hurried over to join us. "You didn't find him then?"

"I'm sorry, Viv," I said. "He wasn't at his place and he never showed up at work either."

"Have you heard anything from the police?" she asked.

"We had a conversation," Harrison said.

"What about? Do they know something?" She sounded frantic, and several of the students glanced our way.

Harry took Viv's arm and led her away from the ears of the students at the first table. There were two elderly women there, who definitely looked like sisters although one was dressed in yellow while the other was in green, both of whom were leaning back in their chairs, trying to hear what was said.

"Inspecteur Lavigne is doing everything he can," Harry said. "Listen, when we stopped by Will's place, we discovered we weren't the first to have been there."

"What do you mean?" Viv frowned.

"His place was ransacked," I said. "It looked like someone was searching for something."

"Oh, no," she said. She put her hand over her mouth. "Who would do such a thing? He's in insurance; surely it can't be that risky of an occupation."

"I don't know," Harrison said. "But my guess is that he has something that somebody else wants. Otherwise why ransack his apartment?"

"But what could it be? The only thing he mentioned to both Scarlett and me was the Renoir landscape that he was trying to authenticate."

"It could be anything," I said. "We should find out what other claims he was working on. Maybe this has nothing to do with the Renoir."

Viv frowned again. "Maybe but I can't help but think that Emile St. James has to have something to do with Will's disappearance. It was too coincidental that Will was grabbed right after an argument with St. James, don't you think?"

Harry and I both shrugged. The truth was that none of us knew Will that well.

"I'm sorry to interrupt, Vivian, but this man insisted upon seeing you," Lucas said from the doorway. We all turned around to face him.

Standing next to him, looking very distraught, was William's boss, Mr. O'Toole.

Chapter 15

"How may I help you?" Vivian asked. She looked bewildered and I knew it was because she was still processing all that had happened and also she had no idea who this man was.

"Good afternoon, Mr. O'Toole," I said. I stepped forward so that his attention turned to me.

Viv turned to look at me, as did Harrison, but I kept my eyes on the round, little man in front of me.

"You." He met my gaze and he flushed with anger. "You did not tell me the truth of your acquaintanceship with William Graham."

I ducked my head. "I'm sorry. It's rather complicated."

"More so than now?" Mr. O'Toole asked. There was heat in his words as if a low-burning anger had boiled them up to the surface. His face was so stiff, even his jowls didn't move. "I believe you have something of mine."

"I'm sorry," I said. "I don't understand."

"Did you steal the Renoir?" he snapped.

"Me?" I gasped. "Wait! What? The Renoir has been stolen?"

"As if you don't know," Mr. O'Toole said. His glare seared me and then Viv. "The two of you, playing Will for a fool. Tell me, did you really think you'd get away with it?"

"Oy! I won't tolerate that sort of talk," Harrison said. He looked furious and Mr. O'Toole took a step back. "Just what are you accusing them of, Mr. O'Toole, was it?"

Now all of Viv's students were staring at our little group. The two older ladies sitting the closest weren't even bothering to pretend that they weren't eavesdropping.

"Perhaps this is not the place for this discussion." Lucas Martin gestured to the open door behind him.

Viv glanced at her class and noticed the two women watching them with their eyes wide and their chins propped on their hands.

"Ella and Marie Porter," Viv scolded. "If you want these hats ready for your return trip to Morse Point, Massachusetts, you'd best get working."

"Nuts, it was just getting interesting, too," the one in yellow hissed to the one in green.

The two elderly ladies exchanged grumpy looks. I noticed that the one dressed in yellow was working on a yellow hat and likewise the one in green a green hat. I suspected these colors were an identity thing for them.

Lucas Martin led the way out of the classroom and back onto the chilly balcony.

"I will monitor your class for you," he said to Viv.

"Thank you, Lucas," she said.

He turned to Mr. O'Toole with one eyebrow raised, and said, "I am quite sure this is a misunderstanding."

Mr. O'Toole waited until Lucas went back inside and then he turned to Viv and studied her. "You are Will's wife?"

"Yes," she said. I noticed there was a slight hesitation but then she nodded as if she was committing to the idea herself.

"And she was with me all last night," I said. "We had dinner with Will and then he brought us back to the office to show us the Renoir, because Viv is an artist and he thought she'd like it. We saw Will get taken right in front of your office. The driver Will had hired for us sped off, and when we demanded that he go back, he dropped us off on some side street. We told the police all of this when we called it in."

"I can vouch for them," Harrison said. "They called me when they were abandoned at the same time that they called the police."

"And who are you?" Mr. O'Toole asked.

"Harrison Wentworth," he said.

I noticed that they didn't shake hands. I also noticed that Mr. O'Toole's eyebrows rose up on his forehead in recognition of the name.

"Aren't you the chap who was accused of murdering Winthrop Dashavoy last fall?" he asked.

"Yes, but now I am one of the partners in Evers and Wentworth, the company formerly known as Carson and Evers," he said.

Mr. O'Toole nodded at him but then frowned at me. He was obviously still annoyed that I had been less than honest the day before. It seemed the only thing to do was to tell him the whole truth, as clearly the police hadn't.

"Listen, I'm sorry I didn't tell you everything about Will and Viv," I said. "I came to your company looking for Will since he and Viv, who is my cousin, are . . . were estranged."

"Were?" he asked.

"We met for dinner last night," Viv said. "We were talking about our marriage and thinking about giving it another try when . . ."

Her voice cracked and she looked distraught. I wrapped an arm about her and shot Mr. O'Toole a dark look.

He rubbed a pudgy hand over his bald head as if hoping to stimulate a reasonable explanation for why all of these awful things were happening.

"Do you see why I didn't tell you?" I asked. "I had to talk to Will first."

He gave an abrupt nod.

"Who do you think stole the Renoir?" Harrison asked. He was frowning. I knew that he was bothered by Mr. O'Toole's assumption that we were involved.

"I cannot believe it was Will. That is why when our security guard told me about the two of you, I assumed you had something to do with it. But I can't ignore the fact that the last recording from our security cameras shows that Will was the last one to go in or out of the vault. After that, the cameras went dead," he said. "Bloody hell, I can't believe this. That man was like a son to me. How could he betray me?"

He looked like he might weep. I felt for him; really I did. But at the same time, I was appalled that he would believe the worst of Will so quickly and without proof.

"But Will was kidnapped," Viv said. "How could you possibly think he had anything to do with the painting being missing if he was abducted? Aren't you worried about him?"

Mr. O'Toole's sad face vanished and he looked at Viv with a sudden clarity that I found alarming. Judging by the way Harrison shifted beside me, he saw it, too.

"Mrs. Graham, how well did you know your husband?" he asked.

Viv's face flashed bright red, and I figured she was either embarrassed to admit that she didn't know him well or she was feeling chastised, which never sat very well with her. There was no denying that her information on her husband was sketchy at best. And she knew it. She sighed.

"Not as well as one would think, I suppose," she said. "Tell me."

"There is a reason William Graham became an investigator—he was very, very good at it."

We all looked at him, wondering what his point was. I mean, of course, Will was good at his job. Why wouldn't he be?

"You don't understand," he said. "Fine art is big business;

therefore, insuring fine art is also big business. William's skills weren't just his knowledge and appreciation of art, rather, he could mix it up with the scariest sort and hold his own."

"You mean he knew how to fight?" Viv asked. Her eyes were wide.

"He knew how to kill if need be," Mr. O'Toole said. Harrison and I exchanged a look. I didn't think it was my imagination that the situation suddenly seemed much more serious than it had this morning.

"William doesn't just investigate claims, he tracks down missing works of art, he mixes and mingles with some of the most disreputable people in all of Europe, and he can handle himself against that sort," Mr. O'Toole said. "He has broken into palaces and stolen back works of art, using nothing more than his wit and his fists. He's also dealt with some of the bottom-feeding scum who steal art and sell it to the highest bidder." Mr. O'Toole lowered his voice, and added, "I have no proof but there is a rumor that he killed a man in Morocco over a cache of paintings missing since the Nazis smuggled them out of France. I am not worried about your husband being abducted, Mrs. Graham."

Viv had gone four shades paler than usual and looked like she might keel over on the spot.

"Was there no sign of a break-in at your building?" Harrison asked.

"No, the side door was left unlocked and someone slipped in, knocked out our security guard and took the painting right out of the vault. I can only assume it was William and an accomplice."

He gave us another beady-eyed stare, which I was finding to be rather tiresome.

"How dare you?" Viv stepped forward now. If anger made his words bubble, it made hers boil over onto the floor with spits and hisses. "Will would never do such a thing. Scarlett and I saw him abducted right in front of your office. Obviously, whoever took him is responsible for taking the painting."

"You don't just 'take' William Graham," Mr. O'Toole argued. "No, there is something wrong about this whole situation."

Then it hit me. In a blinding bit of clarity that I wished I wasn't having because it really was too awful to contemplate, but still if what Mr. O'Toole said was true, that William was a fighter, then it seemed the likeliest possibility.

"Maybe William didn't fight with his abductors for a reason," I said. "Maybe he couldn't fight them because they threatened something he cared about more than the Renoir."

"What could that be?" Viv asked.

We all turned to look at her. It took her a second but she got there.

"Oh," she said. Her voice was soft as if all of the air came out of her on the realization that her husband had likely been threatened and she had been the leverage.

"I hadn't thought of that," O'Toole said grudgingly. "That does make more sense."

"We have to find out who took the painting," Harrison said. "That is the answer to this whole situation. What is the name of the shop where it was purchased?"

O'Toole looked hesitant and Harrison crossed his arms over his chest. It was a posture that signified that he could wait all day if he had to and that he would shake it out of the smaller man if he must.

"This is what I know," O'Toole said. "The painting was originally bought by a man named Jacques Reyer from a *bouquiniste* on the Left Bank. He then took it to his shop in the fourth arrondissement called Boutique Reyer, which sounds elegant but it's really just a secondhand junk shop, where he sold it to a woman, Colette Deneau, who then brought it to us for an appraisal."

"So, Reyer and Deneau are the two people who are insisting that the Renoir belongs to them?" I asked. "Will told us there was some difficulty there."

"Yes, the two of them and the owner of the *bouquiniste*," O'Toole said. He looked tired and irritated all at the same time. "A greedy lot of scoundrels is what they are. My grandfather paid out the insurance on that piece, and it is rightfully ours, damn what the museum and all of these others say."

"The museum is staking a claim as well?" Viv asked.

"They are trying to as is the family of Estelle Brouillard, the woman who bequeathed it to the museum," he said. "Bunch of bloody vultures."

"Viv, I think it is best if you stay here and teach your class," Harrison said. "I'll talk to Lucas and make sure you're safe."

"But I want to help," she protested.

"Viv, if the people who snatched Will are using your safety as leverage, then it is best that you stay here out of sight," I said. "Harry and I will do everything we can to try to find him. And I'm sure Mr. O'Toole will as well."

I directed this last bit at O'Toole, and even though he looked as if he might choke on the words, he agreed with a brusque nod and a muttered, "Of course."

Harrison took a business card out of his pocket and handed it to O'Toole. "If you hear anything, you can contact me at this number."

O'Toole took it and looked at it as if trying to decide if it was authentic or not. He then put it in his coat pocket.

"What are you planning to do?" he asked.

"Talk to everyone who had their hands on that painting," Harrison said. "The painting is the key to finding William, I'm sure of it."

Chapter 16

We left Viv to teach her class, although she looked grumpy about it. O'Toole went back to his office, promising to be in touch if he had any word from William, the police or the people who had taken him.

Harrison checked the time on his watch and then glanced at the sky above. Clouds had moved in over the city and the temperature had dropped. For a moment, I wondered if it was my mood that had brought them in.

"All right, Ginger?" he asked.

"Worried," I said. "About Will and Viv. What a mess."

"Agreed," he said. "But I think you're right. If Will is as wily as O'Toole said, then the only explanation for his abduction is that they must have threatened Viv, leaving him no choice."

"Do you think they'll harm him?" I asked. "I mean, if they've got the painting, why haven't they released him?"

Harrison glanced at me, taking my elbow as he guided me across the street. It was midafternoon now and cars were whizzing past us, honking and screeching their brakes as they raced through the narrow city streets.

"I didn't want to say anything," he said, "but it seems to me that if they are still holding Will, then someone else got the painting first."

"You mean Will could be a hostage?"

Harrison shrugged. "It's just a theory."

I hated to acknowledge it but it sounded like a damn good theory to me.

"I take it we're off to Boutique Reyer?" I asked.

"*Exactement*," he said.

The sexy French accent he used made me shiver but I pretended it was the cold and pulled my coat more tightly about me. The urgency of our situation made me realize that now was not the time to start anything with Harry, which was probably just as well as I really didn't want to spend my life as the butt of my mother's jokes. Two more months, two more months until I was free to date. *Mon Dieu*, I hoped I survived it.

Boutique Reyer was nestled between a *boulangerie* and a *pharmacie* in a block of small shops that sat on the edge of a residential neighborhood. I imagined the foot traffic was good for Reyer as so many people in France bought fresh bread daily.

The smell of warm baked goods wafted out the door as a customer pulled it wide to enter. I almost got sidetracked and followed them inside, but Harrison stayed the course to Reyer's so I did, too. Darn it.

The warmth of the small shop was welcome as we stepped inside. I could feel the heat thaw the end of my nose and the lobes of my ears while I took in the shop, trying to get my bearings.

Harrison took no such time but charged forward toward the counter, looking like he meant business. I followed more slowly as different items caught my attention. The place was full of treasures. You know, *Oh, shiny!* My head whipped back and forth and up and down as I moved past the displays.

A vintage wooden rocking horse, a collection of assorted china, glass stemware, old rugs, a row of elaborate birdcages hanging from the ceiling, a music box with a couple twirling, it all made me feel like I had crawled into Mim's attic to play with her old things.

It struck me then that I hadn't gone into the attic in our place on Notting Hill since I'd returned. When we were younger, Viv and I used to go up there to play dress-up with Mim's old clothes. My favorites were her old Mod dresses from the mid-sixties. She'd even had a pair of white go-go boots that I used to stomp around in. I promised myself upon our return to London, I would go up to the attic and see what was still there.

"*Bon jour, je voudrais parler avec Jacques Reyer, s'il vous plaît,*" Harrison said.

I shook my head in an effort to focus and hurriedly

joined him at the counter. A tall, bony man with thin gray hair combed across his pink scalp and an equally thin mustache-and-goatee combo circling his mouth stood there. He looked as if he was assessing Harrison to see how likely he was to make a sale off him.

"I am Jacques Reyer," he said in English. His accent was thick, and he gave a slight nod of his head as if to say he was comfortable speaking in English.

"How do you do? I'm Harrison Wentworth, and this is Scarlett Parker." He held out his hand and Reyer shook it. He did not shake my hand.

"How can I help you?" Mr. Reyer asked.

"We've come to ask you about the painting, the Renoir," Harrison said.

A look of bitterness pinched Reyer's face like he'd just bitten into an aspirin without a water chaser.

"I do not wish to speak of it," Reyer said. "My shop is closing unless you wish to buy something . . ."

He could have just told us up front that he would say nothing unless we dropped some cash. Suddenly, I wasn't feeling too bad for him about losing the Renoir.

The glass display case in front of us was full of vintage jewelry. A peacock broach was smack dab in the middle, catching my eye with its sparkling green beads. They were the exact same color as Harry's eyes, and they twinkled at me just like his did when I made him laugh.

"How much?" I asked.

Reyer looked down his nose at the piece. "That is a very rare item. One hundred euros."

I felt my eyes bug out of their sockets. At the current

exchange rate that was seventy-five British pounds or one hundred and ten smackers American. For paste beads and a metal I was sure was going to give me a rash, I felt like I should just hand him the money as if he held a gun to my head. I started to refuse but Harry stepped in.

"We'll take it," he said. "Now about the painting—"

"Pay first," the man said. "Cash."

Harrison frowned but reached for his billfold and took out the money. He handed it to the man and the man bagged the bird and handed it to me. Oh, goody, my trip to France was going to be memorialized in a peacock pendant that I was sure we just paid ten times more for than its actual value.

"The painting belongs to me," Reyer said. "And I am going to get it back."

"Yeah," I said. "How do you figure?"

"I am the one who bought it from the *bouquiniste*," he said. "All the bookseller cared about were the books. Pah, the librarian had no idea what she had."

"And you did?" I asked. "You sold the painting for ten euros to a woman named Colette Deneau, correct?"

His goatee trembled with outrage. "That is a lie!"

Harry saw me open my mouth to retort. I don't lie, mostly, and he stepped on my foot. I glared at him but he gave me a look that said to stop speaking. I sighed but complied.

"How did it happen that this Colette Deneau managed to purchase the painting from you?" Harry asked.

"She tricked me, that's how!" Reyer raised his pointer finger up in the air as he spoke.

I felt the weight of the peacock pin in my hand and felt his pain, really, I did.

"How did she trick you?" Harrison asked.

"She told me she was an art student and that the painting while lovely was clearly a fraud," he said. His previous sour expression returned to his face. "She pointed out brushstrokes and said the signature was wrong, but it wasn't. She lied to me and told me the painting was junk. Like a fool, I believed her instead of my own knowledge."

"But how did she con you?" I asked. "If you are so knowledgeable, that is?"

Yes, I was being rude. So what, he was a pompous jackass who had just soaked us for over a hundred bucks.

"Quite simply," he said. "I am a Frenchman and she . . ." His voice trailed off and then he whistled and made an hourglass shape with his hands. "I did not stand a chance."

I rolled my eyes. Men!

"Still, the painting belongs to the insurance company," Harry said. "They paid a claim on its theft over forty years ago."

Reyer's whole head turned an ugly shade of red. "The painting is mine! I will not rest until the courts deem it is so!"

"But—" Harry began but Reyer cut him off.

"Out!" he cried. "The two of you out! Before I call the police or toss you out with my own hands."

We exchanged a look. Was he serious? Reyer looked to weigh less than I did. Reyer reached for a cell phone resting on the counter between us. So, it was to be the police then.

"No need to show us the way," Harry said. Then he grabbed my hand and dragged me out the door.

We jogged an entire block before slowing to a walk. I was gulping cold air and laughing while my hand was still enfolded in his. When we paused to catch our breath, I made a whistling noise like Reyer and let go of his hand to make an hourglass with my hands.

"Really?" I asked. "Did he really do that?"

Harry busted out a laugh and said, "I think our friend was clearly out of his league."

Harry's cheeks were ruddy from the cold. His green eyes bright in the half light that comes with early evening in winter. His lips were parted and his teeth a slash of white. I had a sudden urge to wrap myself up in his smile like it was a blanket on a cold winter's day.

It hit me then that even while running from a crazy Frenchman in the heart of winter in Paris, when I was with Harry, it was fun. Ridiculously fun, in fact. And like a snowball to the temple, it hit me. I was in love with Harrison Wentworth.

"What?" he asked. "Do I have a bogie hanging out of my nose?"

He ran his gloved hand under his nose and I blinked.

"Uh, no," I said. "Sorry. I just got lost in thought there for a second."

"Solving the case of the missing painting or the missing man?" he asked.

"Both," I said. I forced a lightness into my voice that I did not feel. "You know what an overachiever I am."

"That I do," he said. He casually draped an arm over

my shoulders and said, "I don't think Reyer knows anything. Let's go back to the school and collect Viv. I don't want her out and about on her own."

"Agreed," I said.

His arm brought warmth and security and my insides heated up to boiling at having him so close. There was nothing I wanted more in the world than to turn toward him and kiss him. I could hear my mother saying *I told you so* in my head in a maddening singsong voice that was designed specifically to torture me.

No, I could not give in. Two more months, whether I was in love with him or not. I was. But that made it even worse, because knowing how I felt made the stakes even higher. I desperately did not want to get hurt again. Darn it!

"We'd better hurry if we want to catch her," I said.

I eased out from under his arm, trying to look casual about it. If he noticed, it didn't show. I picked up our pace to a half jog and he fell in beside me as if matching his longer gait to my lesser one was as natural as breathing.

Oh, Harry, why now? Why did I have to have the "I'm in love with you" epiphany now, in Paris, when I couldn't do anything about it? This was so unfair.

As we hustled by a patisserie, I promised myself several disgustingly delicious, flaky, puffy, gooey desserts as a reward. Later.

We took Viv to dinner at a local brasserie near our apartment. She insisted she wasn't hungry but Harrison was not to be deterred. Since *brasserie* also means brewery, he ordered beer for all three of us as well as a charcuterie board.

When the food arrived, I found I was starving. The large wedges of homemade toast rubbed with olive oil and minced garlic were the perfect accompaniment to the charcuterie board, which was literally a huge cutting board, loaded with a selection of cured meats, such as salami, prosciutto, pâté, bacon, duck sausages and some sort of fruit-based chutney that was a nice respite from all of the salty meat.

I loaded my plate and nibbled while Harrison caught Viv up on our interview with Reyer. She had begun the evening looking unhappy. She didn't eat but downed one pint of dark ale and asked for another. Harry shot me a worried look but I shrugged. Having never been married and had my estranged husband abducted, I wasn't really in a position to judge her current behavior.

Besides, I was still reeling from my own epiphany, but instead of anesthetizing my shock with beer, I was going with meat. Bacon really can cure whatever ails you, I was pretty sure.

"Excuse me, Mademoiselle." Our waiter appeared beside our table. He was addressing Vivian and both Harry and I watched as he handed her a note. "A gentleman asked me to deliver this to you."

"Thank you," Viv said. As soon as he walked away, she hissed, "Maybe it's from Will."

Harry looked grim and I knew he was thinking the same thing I was, that it was most likely from whoever took Will. I swallowed my bite of bacon and it went down hard, scraping my throat as it dragged a knot of dread down with it.

"It's from that man, Emile St. James," Viv said. Her voice and her hands were shaking but I couldn't tell if it was fear or anger making them do so. When she glanced up, her blue eyes were fierce. Okay, it was anger. "He wants to talk. We are to meet at a cemetery at ten o'clock."

She leapt to her feet, almost knocking her chair to the ground. Harry caught it before it clattered. When he righted it, he took Viv's arm, holding her in place.

"Wait, you have plenty of time," he said. "May I see the note before you take off?"

She thrust it at him and then turned and pulled on her coat. It was clear that she was planning to rush out and go meet St. James. I glanced at the charcuterie and sighed. So much bacon, so little time.

"You're not going alone," I said.

"The note was to me," Viv argued. "What if he has Will and he will only talk to me?"

"We'll deal with that when we face him," Harrison said. He waved to our waiter, who came over. "We need to leave. Can you box this for us?"

The waiter nodded, even more vigorously when Harry handed him what looked to be a substantial tip. I knew the French considered doggy bags an affront to dining etiquette, but given that their government was trying to combat the country's immense food wastage by mandating that take-away boxes be provided upon request, I wondered if they were rethinking their feelings on the matter. Our waiter arrived back in minutes, so clearly he had no issue with it.

Harrison paid the bill and I took the leftovers. We exited the restaurant behind Viv, who walked with a decided swagger, looking like she was gearing up for a fight. Either it was the beer or the anger or both, making her ready to rumble. Oh, boy.

Chapter 17

We stopped by our apartment first. Suzette was in the front parlor with some of the other tenants, so we waved on our way up to our apartment but didn't linger for an after-dinner drink.

Harrison instructed us to dress warmly while he figured out the best way to get to the cemetery to meet St. James. Viv and I both dressed casually in jeans and thick wool sweaters and sturdy walking boots as opposed to the fashionable ones we'd been traipsing around in.

By the time we joined Harry, he had changed as well. He was in jeans and a thick sweater. He had a slouchy hat on his head and a scarf around his neck. He looked adorable. My insides melted a little and I quickly glanced away. It would not do for him to see how I felt about him. I was barely comfortable with it myself, never mind letting him get a glimpse of it.

A terrified part of me wondered what was going to happen in two months when we did start dating. What if I was in love with him, but he really just liked me a lot? What if he never fell as hard as I had apparently fallen? It could be a disaster. My heart could get squashed. Suddenly, I felt like all of that bacon was going to make a return appearance.

"All right, Ginger?" he asked. He frowned at me as he studied my face. "You look a bit peaky."

And there it was, his cute British way of speaking that always took me out at the knees. I was doomed! Doomed, I tell ya!

"She's fine, let's go," Viv snapped.

Well, if that wasn't a splash of cold water, I don't know what was.

"I might not be fine," I protested. "That bacon could have been tainted."

"Well, then perhaps you shouldn't have eaten four pounds of it," she said.

"Ah!" I gasped.

Abruptly, Viv looked stricken and she cried, "I'm sorry! I'm sorry! I'm just . . . oh, God, I'm a bloody mess!"

I opened my arms and she stepped into them for a big, bracing, cousinly hug. I glanced over her shoulder at Harry and he gave me a warm smile. Yeah, I couldn't blame Viv for being short with me. If someone abducted Harry, I would punch through bricks to find him if need be.

"It's all right," I said. "We'll find him. We will."

Viv nodded and sniffed and then led the way out the door.

Harry pulled me back when I went to follow her. His gaze met mine and his eyes were warm as he said, "You really are one of the nicest people I've ever known."

He kissed my forehead in a gesture that was very sweet but a little too sibling-like for my taste at the moment. Still, its impact rocked my foundation so I wisely said nothing but just nodded and followed Viv out the door, wondering how I was going to survive the next two months without tackling Harry to the ground and having my way with him.

"Why a graveyard?" Viv asked as we walked from the Metro stop to the designated meeting place, which was the famous Père Lachaise Cemetery, known for the graves of Oscar Wilde, Jim Morrison, and Maria Callas, among others. "I mean, how are we going to find him amidst all these graves? Oh, no, you don't think he's killed Will already, do you?"

"No," Harrison said. "The graveyard closed hours ago; most of them do at six o'clock. I think this is just a scare tactic to give you a fright."

"It's working," I said.

The street was deserted, making the creep factor high. Tall trees loomed over the sidewalk that ran along the perimeter of the graveyard nestled in the twentieth arrondissement. Shadows shifted under the streetlights, and I knew if anyone so much as brushed by me unexpectedly,

I was going to do a screaming jump scare that might just raise some of the dead.

"I imagine we will find him parked at the entrance," Harrison said.

He gestured up ahead, and sure enough, a sleek black car sat in front of the large stone walls that were cordoned off by small stone barricades with chains roped in between them. I wondered who they were trying to keep out or if they were trying to keep someone in.

"Why, that miserable son of a bitch," Viv snarled.

She strode forward at a clip before Harrison or I could grab her. She went straight up to the car and rapped on the passenger window, and because her fingers were gloved, they made a disturbing thumping sound, you know, sort of like you'd expect it to sound if someone was knocking on the inside of a casket. I shivered.

"Get out!" Viv cried. "Get out here and face me like a man, you miserable troll."

Abruptly, all the doors to the car popped open and several bulky men, who looked like they broke fingers and more substantial body parts for a living, stepped out. *Eep!*

The driver moved stiffly to the only door that remained closed. With great patience, he waited for Viv to move aside before he opened the door. She took a reluctant step back and I knew it was because she didn't want to appear intimidated.

She didn't have to. I'm sure my bug-eyed glance at the scary group was doing a fine job of it for her. I tried to look nonchalant and failed miserably as I mentally scanned the different ways that they could do us in. Would they shoot us? Cut us up like fish bait? We were near a cemetery—maybe they were planning to bury us alive. A small whimper escaped my lips.

"Steady, Ginger," Harry whispered. It was as if he knew exactly where my dark thoughts had taken me.

The bespoke pant leg of a suit and a very stylish designer men's shoe appeared out of the car followed by another leg and the rest of the suit, which cost probably more than we made in a month at the hat shop, and in case you don't know, custom hats are very expensive and we do quite well.

"Mrs. Graham," Emile St. James said to Viv. He didn't bother to acknowledge Harry or me. "You are as lovely as your husband described."

"You have William?" Viv asked.

She stepped forward but two of the henchmen stepped in front of her. Their resemblance to the stone wall guarding the tombs behind us was uncanny.

"Is he all right?" Viv asked. "Tell me where he is. Tell me!"

Viv was losing her temper. Usually that was me, so it was interesting to step back and witness it. She looked quite glorious with her blond hair flying, her brows arched over her bright blue eyes, her nostrils flaring and her hands tightening into fists.

Emile St. James seemed to think so, too. He looked Viv over in a way that made my skin crawl. It was smarmy and seedy, and if we didn't need him for information, I would have punched him in the mouth.

"Funny," he said. "I was going to ask you the same thing."

"I don't know where he is," Viv said.

"No matter," St. James said. "I'll happily take the painting instead."

"You think I have the painting?" Viv asked. "Why would I?"

"Because your devoted husband gave it to you," he said. He reached out a hand to touch one of Viv's long curls, the one that was hanging just over her right breast.

"Hey!" I cried.

"Oy!" Harrison yelled.

Emile St. James ignored us and picked up the curl, running it between his fingers as if admiring the soft, silky texture. Viv jerked her head in the other direction, yanking the curl away from him. I saw her wince and knew that he had held on tight just to hurt her. I wanted to slug him right in his weasely little face or his soft man parts, whatever I could reach first.

I took a step forward to stand at Viv's side and one of his goons grabbed me. His big meat hooks wrapped around my chest and he lifted me off the ground.

"Hey!" I protested and kicked my legs at his shins as hard as I could. When he grunted, I was pleased that my clunky boots had nice thick heels.

Harrison spun toward us and punched the man right in the side of the head. He went slack and dropped me and I stumbled into Harrison's arms. The comfort was short-lived as another of St. James's thugs grabbed Harrison and plowed a fist into his side, forcing the air out of him with an *oomph*.

Viv cried out and helped me steady him. Harrison

shook his head and launched himself at the man, and then next thing I knew, they were exchanging blows. They were equally matched, but Harrison was clearly the better fighter, dodging blows and hitting the man with solid punches, until another man grabbed Harry from behind, trapping his arms behind his back and letting his assailant hammer at him with punches to the gut and a right hook to his jaw.

"Harry!" I cried. I went to jump forward but one of the men grabbed my arm.

"Stop it!" Viv demanded.

"Tell me where the painting is!" St. James demanded. His face turned red and he looked a bit demented.

"I don't know!" she yelled. "Don't you think I would tell you if I knew?"

"Then you will die," St. James said.

"And when Will comes looking for his wife, and she is dead, then you really won't be able to catch him. Great plan," I said. My voice was scathing in its contempt as I tugged and yanked, trying to get free of the thug who held me. "Harm us and Viv will disappear, leaving you with no way to find Will. Harm Viv, and Will has no reason to come back here. Will is the only one who knows who has the painting. Do you really want to kill your only chance of finding it?"

Viv looked at St. James and tipped up her chin as if to say that everything I said, which was a big bluff by the way, was true.

St. James stared at her for a long while, then he flicked his wrist and the man holding Harrison let him go as did the man I was twisting against. I stumbled into Harry and his arms came around me as blood poured from a gash over his eye. Rage pumped through me, and it was all I could do not to wrap my fingers around St. James's throat and squeeze with all my might.

Frosty air was sawing in and out of my lungs, burning my throat. I didn't give in to the urge to attack the vile man in front of me. Instead, I hugged Harry close, relieved that he was all right and that St. James looked like he was reconsidering having us killed.

Instead, he turned a half-lidded gaze in Viv's direction and said, "This isn't over."

And just like that, he and his entourage of jerkwads left us standing in the street and, in Harrison's case, bleeding.

Chapter 18

Suzette greeted us at the door with a gasp.

"What happened?" she cried. "Were you attacked?"

She looked past us out into the dark night as if the shadows were waiting to take another swipe at us.

"Long story," I said.

Suzette pulled us into the drawing room. It was free of other guests, thank goodness. The fire was crackling and a decanter was sitting on a tray with glasses. I wondered if it would be considered bad form to drink right out of the bottle.

The cab ride home had been tense, as Harrison bled, Viv and I shook, and the cab driver cast us surreptitious glances as if he feared we were about to rob him, or worse.

Viv and I led Harrison to the couch while Suzette disappeared to get some first aid supplies. Viv reached for the decanter as I unfastened Harrison's jacket. He looked at me and gave me a half smile as if to reassure me, but all it did was make me want to cry.

"Thanks for what you did tonight," I said, low so only he could hear me. "You know, for looking out for me."

He reached up and cupped my cheek. The look in his eyes was steadfast and true and stole what little breath I had left in my lungs.

"Always," he said.

"A hot washcloth, ointment and bandages," Suzette said as she came dashing back into the room. "Did I forget anything? Oh, how about a pain reliever?"

She dropped the items into my lap and dashed back out of the room.

"I think we've got her all in a fizz," Viv said. Then she downed a shot of single malt scotch in one gulp.

"I'll take one of those," Harrison said.

"Me, too," I said.

We clinked glasses and tossed it back. It was like inhaling a fireball. I blew out a breath but the fire inside didn't go out, it just slowly unfurled to my extremities, leaving a pleasing warmth and making my post-traumatic shakes subside.

I set to work on Harrison's gash. All in all, he'd gotten pretty lucky that St. James's posse of evil hadn't broken his nose or worse.

He flinched the first time I applied a little pressure, trying to clean out the wound, but he settled down once Viv handed him another shot before she started pacing around the room. She was clearly still agitated but had stopped drinking, opting to do laps around the furniture instead. Smart girl.

"Don't get shnockered on me now," I said to Harrison. "I don't think I can heft you up all those flights of stairs."

My face was just an inch from his and I felt his gaze on my lips. His smile was crooked and he said, "Oh, I could make it up those stairs on my own, no matter how much I drank, with proper motivation."

It did not take a mind reader to know what he considered proper motivation. I felt my face get warm.

"Behave," I whispered, although to be truthful, I didn't really want him to. Tonight had been terrifying, and being distracted by him and this thing between us helped calm me down and get me centered again.

"Here you go." Suzette came back bearing a glass of water and a couple of Nurofen tablets.

Nurofen is the French equivalent to ibuprofen, and Harrison tossed them back, using the scotch instead of the water. I took the water from Suzette and swapped it for the scotch in Harrison's hand. He looked longingly after the little glass of amber liquid but drank the water. I felt for him—being an adult is a bit of a drag sometimes.

Suzette sat down in one of the armchairs and poured herself a glass from the decanter. She sipped it like a lady while Viv continued to pace around the room and I rubbed ointment onto Harry's cut. I held up the small adhesive bandage but he shook his head.

"We have to find Will," Viv said. She sounded distraught. I really couldn't blame her, especially with someone like St. James looking for him.

"We will," Harrison said. He sounded so certain of it that I almost believed him, which I'm sure was his intent.

"Please, what happened?" Suzette asked.

We told her about our day, each of us filling in with bits and pieces until the entire story was told.

Suzette glanced at each of us in turn and then finished her drink in one swallow. "*Mon Dieu*, you were lucky to not have been killed."

We were all silent for a moment, absorbing the truth of her words. What would it have been like to have been slain on the streets of Paris? The thought made me tremble.

Harrison put his hand on my back. The warmth seeped in through my clothes. It patted down the fear that still sparked inside me, extinguishing it completely. I turned and gave him a closed-lipped smile of gratitude.

"The painting is obviously the key," I said. My voice was gruff and I cleared my throat. "If we can figure out who took the painting, then we can find Will."

"Clearly, it isn't the shop owner, Reyer," Harrison said. "He was too angry at the loss of the painting and he didn't strike me as being smart enough to figure out how to get it."

"And it's not St. James," I added. "If he had Will or the painting, he wouldn't have come after us."

"Who does that leave then?" Viv asked.

"What about the family who originally bequeathed the painting to the museum?" Suzette asked. "Would they want it back?"

"Or the woman who bought it from Reyer and took it to O'Toole's," I said. "What was her name, Colette Deneau?"

"That's who we'll talk to first thing in the morning," Harrison said. "And if she doesn't have any answers for us, then we'll talk to the family of the woman who left the painting to the museum. Do we know her name?"

"Yes," Viv said. "Will mentioned it when he showed us the painting. It was a lady named Estelle Brouillard and she left the painting to the Musée de l'Or."

"Do you think we should talk to someone at the museum as well?" I asked. My thinking being that we should not leave any leads unfollowed.

"Let's start with Ms. Deneau and work from there," Harrison said. "First thing in the morning."

I nodded.

"I'm coming with you," Viv said. "As Will's wife, I might be able to convince her to tell you more than she would on her own."

Harrison shook his head. "St. James is going to be watching you. You need to remain at the school, where we know you're safe and where he will be occupied keeping an eye on you."

"But—" Viv started to protest.

"He's right," Suzette interrupted. "And not only that, but if your husband does try to make contact, he will likely look for you at the school."

"Plus, your students need you," I added. "It's not like Mr. Martin can just find another milliner."

Viv glanced between us. Then she heaved a sigh and said, "I hate this."

"I know," I said. I stood up and hugged her. "It will be impossible for us to move about the city undetected if you're with us, so even though I know this is hard, it really is for the best."

Viv nodded. "Still hate it."

Harrison rose from his seat with a wince and a cringe and hugged us both. "We'll get this sorted. Don't worry."

Maybe it was just wishful thinking on my part, but I believed him.

Viv left the house with Lucas the next morning while Harry and I strategized over breakfast. This was the first morning I made it downstairs when the other tenants were about and I realized Suzette really did have a full house.

The former hospitality professional in me was quite impressed with her operation. She likely made a tidy living renting out apartments in the heart of Paris. Mostly, it was foreigners doing quick vacation rentals and I heard several different languages buzz in my ear as I sipped my coffee.

"I'm having no luck turning up an address for Colette Deneau," Harry said.

"Back to Boutique Reyer?" I asked. "You know he is just going to be thrilled to see us."

"Can't be helped," Harrison said. "He is the only one besides the people at O'Toole Insurance who dealt with Colette Deneau, and of the two I think he is the more likely to help us."

"Aren't you an optimist? I wonder what overpriced doodad he is going to coerce us into buying today?" I asked.

I reached into my purse where the peacock pin was still in its bag and put it on the table.

Harry grinned at me. "It really is the ugliest broach I've seen. What made you choose it?"

"I . . . er . . . uh," I stammered. He caught me off guard with that one.

"What an interesting broach," Suzette said. She arrived at our table with a coffeepot. She glanced at it and then at Harry. "It's the same color as your eyes."

She held up the pot but we both shook our heads. With a smile, she left us to flit to the next table. When I looked at Harry, he was grinning at me.

I could feel a hot red rash creep up my neck to my face. Damn pale skin. I probably looked like I was on fire. Still, I tried to bluff.

I held up the pin and squinted at it and then at Harry, skirting eye contact by keeping my gaze moving.

"Huh, fancy that," I said. "She's right."

His grin broadened. I didn't fool him one little bit.

"Is that why you chose it?" he asked. His voice was a deep rough rasp in his sexy British accent. Yes, even after all these months, it still made me dizzy.

"Maybe," I said. "Or perhaps I just like the color green, or peacocks, yeah, come to think of it, I'm really fond of those screechy birds."

He lifted his coffee cup to his lips and drained it. When he put the cup down, he stared me straight in the eye. His look was anticipatory, as if he was waiting for something.

"All right, fine," I said. The steady stare forced the truth out of me like a crowbar wrenching open a locked door. "It did remind me of your eyes. There, satisfied?"

The look he gave me scorched. "Not. Even. Close."

Oh, my!

The cold air felt good on my overheated skin. Because time was of the essence, we hired a cab to take us to Reyer's shop. Sitting next to Harry in the cab made me entirely too aware of his heat, his scent, his solid build. We had spent more time together in the past thirty-six hours than we had in weeks. It made it very hard to friend zone him, much as I tried.

"All right, Ginger?" he asked.

"Good, I'm good," I lied.

The cab pulled up to the curb with a sharp stop, and I saw Harry grimace as he was slammed back into the seat.

"Still hurts, huh?" I asked.

"I'm just a little stiff from sleeping on the couch," he said.

I shook my head at him. I had seen him changing his shirt that morning, another thing that made the friend thing virtually impossible as I'm pretty sure friends didn't gawk at friends when they were half dressed, and I saw the bruising on his side and his ribs. The punishment he had taken last night had been severe and yet here he was, back to helping Viv and me find William. In all my life I don't think I'd ever met a man as purely good as Harry. Again, I was swamped by my feelings for him.

"You're a terrible liar," I said.

He paid the cabbie and held the door open for me. "Takes one to know one."

"Is that the best you've got?" I asked.

He gave me a half smile. "Today it is."

As we approached Reyer's shop, I noticed that it looked dark. That couldn't be good. I really didn't want to have to cool our heels, waiting for him to open.

Harrison tugged the door handle. It was unlocked and opened easily. He looked puzzled and gestured for me to wait while he went in. Honestly, it's like he didn't know me at all. I trotted in behind him, ignoring the frown he sent my way.

"Hello?" Harry called out.

The only sound was the ticking of a large clock in the corner.

"Mr. Reyer?" I cried. Still nothing.

"Wait here," Harrison said. "I'm going to see if I can find a light switch."

"Okay," I said. Mostly, because the shapes and shadows creeped me out. I could feel the hair on the back of my neck standing on end.

There was a bad smell to the shop. It hadn't smelled like this yesterday. It made my stomach hurt and my eyes water. Unconsciously, I began to walk back toward the door, craving fresh air.

The lights snapped on and the shadows evaporated except for one. Creeping out across the floor, from behind a bucket of colorful paper parasols, was a deep crimson puddle.

Chapter 19

A shriek broke the silence. It took me a second to realize it had come from my mouth, then I started shaking. Sadly, I had stumbled upon ominous red pools before in my life and it never turned out well.

Harrison spun around from his spot by the wall, and I pointed. My hand was shaking so hard I tucked it back against my side. We both stepped forward toward the blood. Yes, I knew it was blood just like I knew there was going to be a body nearby.

Harrison got there first. He knelt beside Reyer and checked his outstretched hand for a pulse. He put his ear to the man's chest, but really there was no point. Reyer was dead.

Jacques Reyer's sightless eyes were gazing up at the ceiling, his mouth was slack, his body seemed cold and stiff. I didn't want to look, but it seemed disrespectful not to acknowledge the man's passing. The pool of blood seeped out from under his head and I could only assume that he had been bludgeoned by something in his own shop. I glanced around the floor until I saw a brass statuette of a woman in a toga, holding a basketful of grapes. There was a tuft of gray hair on the basket as well as congealed blood.

I felt my stomach roll and I lurched back away from the smell of death and did some serious mouth breathing.

Harrison joined me. I turned toward him, looking for a hug of comfort, but he blew past me into the back of the shop. Huh?

I grabbed my phone out of my purse. We needed to call the police, an ambulance, the consulate? I was unclear.

"Harrison, where are you going?" I asked. "I need you to do the talking."

I frowned at my phone. Viv had told me the number for emergencies in France. I hadn't committed it to memory as what were the odds I would need that information again? I tried to remember but my head was fuzzy and I still felt ill.

I hurried toward the back of the shop where Harrison had disappeared and found him in what must have been Reyer's office. He was searching the man's desk.

"What are you doing?" I asked. "We have to call the police."

"We will just as soon as I find what I'm looking for," he said.

"What are you looking for?"

"Colette Deneau's address," he said. His voice was grim.

"Good thinking."

I hurried around the desk and started to help him. Reyer was not a tidy man and his desk was covered in odds and ends. A closed laptop computer, pens, pencils, a magnifying glass, scissors, a calculator, all of the things that helped him do his job as the seller of secondhand treasures.

My chest felt tight as I realized he wouldn't be using any of this stuff ever again. He hadn't been very pleasant to us yesterday, but he certainly didn't deserve this horrible end.

"Do you think someone was trying to rob the place?" I asked.

"No," Harrison answered. He had moved on to the desk drawers and was sifting through the contents.

"Then who—" I began but he interrupted.

"Search now, chat later, Ginger," he said.

He sounded worried. It made me nervous and I began to check over the desk again, looking for anything that had the name "Colette Deneau." There was nothing. I read all of the scraps of paper but there was nothing with her name.

Beside the phone was an article clipped from the evening newspaper *Le Monde*. I wouldn't have noticed it except for the fact that several lines in the article were underlined, one of which included the name "Colette Deneau," and an address was scribbled in the margin. It had to be for her.

"I found something!" I cried.

Harrison looked at me and I held out the paper to him.

He scanned the article, which, judging from the little I could understand of it, was the story about the Renoir being bought by Colette Deneau and how it turned out to be a missing painting worth a fortune.

It occurred to me how frustrating that must have been for Reyer. Here he was, a man of collectibles, and he stumbles upon a painting that is sold to him for nothing so he assumes that it has little value and then he sells it for even less to a woman who obviously knew she had found something. It had to be galling. No wonder he had been so curt with us.

"Excellent!" Harrison said. "Now we can pay her a visit."

"After we call the police," I said.

I was feeling very guilty for leaving Reyer's body unattended. It seemed heartless somehow. Harrison squeezed my shoulder with one of his big man hands.

"There was nothing we could have done for him," he said.

"Should we slip out the back?" I asked. "The front door is unlocked. We could call it in when we're away from here or let someone else discover the body."

He stared at me.

"Okay, fine," I said. "That would be pretty lousy, but I'm a little worried about what Inspecteur Lavigne will think of us."

"It's a concern," he agreed. "But if there are any security cameras or a CCTV around here, we're already on film and I don't relish explaining to the police why we chose to do a runner."

"Good point," I said. "Can you call the police? I will go stand by the door and make sure no one else comes in."

He used his phone to snap a picture of the article before putting it back down on the desk, and I went out front. I was very careful not to look at Reyer as I passed. I knew that I was going to have nightmares for weeks about this one. The man had been alive yesterday and now he wasn't. Just like that, life could be snatched, or in his case clobbered away. It made me a bit dizzy to think about it.

I watched people hurry past on their way to work, off to see the sights, gazing into the windows they passed with no idea that death lurked so close by. I fervently hoped no one was going to stop in at the shop. I didn't want to have to explain about the man lying on the floor just a few feet away from me. I hugged my middle trying to ease my shakes.

The police who came to the scene treated us as if we were poor unfortunate tourists who happened to be at the wrong place at the wrong time, and we let them. We gave them an exact accounting of what had transpired except for the part about searching Reyer's office, natch.

After an hour of questions intermingled with waiting, we gave the inspector who arrived our information and we were free to go. There was no question that Harrison being a well-respected businessman and fluent in French helped us tremendously.

"What do we do now?" I asked.

"We are going to find Ms. Deneau and talk to her," Harrison said as we left Boutique Reyer.

He was tapping on his phone and I imagined he was searching for her location on a map. I had a million questions, like, were we going to tell her about Reyer? Were we going to pretend to be someone else and keep our identities a secret? If we were, maybe we could pretend to be man and wife. I shook my head, yeah, no, that was a different daydream.

Focus, Scarlett. I mentally slapped myself.

Without looking up from his phone, Harrison grabbed my hand. "We need to catch the Metro, come on!"

I let him drag me down the street toward the Metro stop. While the Paris Metro was fine, I have to admit that I missed the London Underground. I missed having a voice tell me to mind the gap in a language I understood, and I missed giggling like a dumb American every time I rode the line that ended at Cockfoster's. Yes, it's a real stop, and ever since I bumped into two American boys on the Piccadilly line, snickering over the name, I've never been able to keep a straight face when I see it on the board or hear it called out as the stop.

Once we were in the station, we used our passes to access the platforms. Harrison studied the map, while I stood beside him, having no idea where we were going. It occurred to me that this week would have been much more difficult, and possibly deadly in the case of Emile St. James, without him.

"Are we taking the Metro or the RER?" I asked. There are two train systems in Paris, as I had learned when I got lost briefly on my first day here.

"The Metro," he said. "The address we're looking for

is in an old neighborhood on the Right Bank, so we'll have to change trains to get there. Come on, I think I've got it."

As if it were perfectly natural, he took my hand in his and we hurried to the platform. I had to admit, I liked that he felt the need to take my hand, especially as it wasn't peak season and the Paris Metro was nowhere near as hot or crowded as it got in the summertime.

We hurried along the white-tiled tunnel until we got to the platform. The sign overhead flashed the estimated time of our train. I had to give the Paris Metro serious props for its punctuality. If it said it would be here in several moments, it would.

While we waited for the white and green train to arrive, I squeezed Harrison's hand in mine. He glanced from the tunnel to me and I smiled at him.

"I'm really glad you're here," I said.

His returning smile glowed like the sun just tipping the horizon.

"Me, too," he said.

I felt the warmth of his affectionate gaze all the way down to my squishy center. Luckily, the train chose that moment to arrive, before I did something really dumb like throw myself at him.

The train stopped and Harrison unlatched the door so we could step inside. There were several people already on board but we managed to grab two seats. I noted that Harrison was still holding my hand and I let him.

There was no denying that it gave me great comfort given the morning's events. Images of the pool of blood seeping out from under Jacques Reyer's head made me queasy. A few years ago the sight would have sent me into a panicked, dry-heaving, eyes-rolling-back-in-my-head sort of tizzy, but now I was different.

Partly, I knew it was because the man beside me was keeping me centered and balanced. It was hard to go off the deep end when you had a solid rock to which to cling. But I also knew it was because ever since I had arrived in London, crazy things had happened. People had been poisoned, stabbed, thrown off roofs and strangled. It struck me then that maybe I was becoming desensitized to death. The thought horrified me.

"Ginger, hello? You in there?"

I turned to find Harrison frowning at me with concern.

"Sorry, what?" I asked.

"You all right?" he asked. "You look a bit knackered."

"I'm all right," I said. "But . . ."

He leaned forward, encouraging me to finish my sentence.

"Do you think it's possible that there's something about me that makes all of these horrible things happen?" I asked. Yeah, I knew it was a dumb question, still . . .

"No! God, no," he said. "It's just been a really weird year."

"I just feel like every time I turn around, someone is getting murdered, and it does seem to be every time I turn around, why do I always have to find the body?" I asked. My voice was getting higher with each word until I was pretty sure I was squeaking as loudly as the one train wheel that always seemed to lack sufficient grease.

Harrison let go of my hand and put his arm around my shoulders. "I think you might be in a bit of shock."

I leaned against him. I didn't care if proximity made it even more difficult to keep him in the friend zone; right now I needed comfort.

"The fact is we have no idea who Reyer dealt with on a regular basis," he said. "We are busy trying to figure out what happened to William and a painting, and maybe Reyer's death had something to do with that but likely not. He dealt with loads of people and volumes of stuff. His death could be completely unrelated to our search."

I nodded. He was right. Given how much Reyer had made us pay for the peacock broach, who knew if he'd done the same to someone else and that person had come back in a fit and clocked him with his own statuette.

"This is us," Harrison said.

We moved to stand in front of the door while the train was still moving. There was an urgency to underground travel that made me a teensy bit anxious. It was all about catching the train, getting on the train, getting off the train, all at top speed, no lollygagging. It was unfortunate because really I could have an advanced degree in lollygagging, I was that good at it.

As soon as the train stopped, Harrison unlatched the door and we stepped out. We had to catch another train from the platform and I followed him, yes, still holding hands, as this station was much more crowded than the last.

The interesting thing about being underground is that when I ride the escalator to the *Sortie*, French for "Exit," I find that when I step back outside into the sunlight, I have lost all sense of time. I knew it was now around midday, but it felt weird as if my time underground had erased an hour or two of my life, which was ridiculous because we hadn't been down there that long.

"This way," Harrison said. We left the large Metro stop behind us as we walked along the busy street. "We are headed to the Marais."

"My French is rusty, I know," I said. "But doesn't that mean 'swamp'?"

"Marsh, actually," he said. "Centuries ago, this area of Paris used to flood, but it has long been a favorite of aristocrats, and it was revitalized in the sixties and is considered quite hip now."

As we worked our way onto the smaller, quieter streets of the third arrondissement, I noted the exclusive-looking townhomes and pretty streets and wished that I were here for any other reason than to track down a missing cousin-in-law and a rare and valuable painting.

"Here," Harrison said. He pushed through an iron gate into the courtyard of a large red brick building. On the lower patio there were several stone benches and raised flower beds that were presently barren.

There were two main doors on the lower floor and Harrison glanced at them and then shook his head. Still holding my hand, he led me up the staircase to the upper level. Again, there were two doors. One was painted a rich red, much like the brickwork around it, while the other was sunflower yellow, cheery and optimistic, especially in this January gloom.

"There, that one," Harrison said, pointing to the yellow door. I hoped this was a sign that Colette was friendly.

We paused in front of her door, listening. I didn't hear anything and leaned back and shook my head at Harrison. He nodded, his expression grim.

He let go of my hand and rapped on the door. It was thick wood and the sound echoed in the quiet courtyard. We waited for several seconds but no one answered. He knocked again. This time I heard someone moving inside.

I saw the curtain in the window by the door move and I got the feeling we were being checked out. I tried to look as innocent as possible; this was actually harder to do once I thought about it. I smiled in the direction of the window, hoping I didn't scare her away.

I heard the lock on the door being undone and took it as a good sign. A woman I would guess about my age answered the door. She was pretty with an upturned nose and full lips, a heart-shaped face framed by thick blond waves. Her figure was all lush curves, which certainly matched the description Reyer had given with his wolf whistle of appreciation.

"*Bonjour, Mademoiselle*," Harry said.

I saw the girl look him over like he was a tasty crème brûlée. I moved in more closely so that she'd have to register my presence whether she liked it or not. A little frown appeared when her gaze turned toward me. So that would be not, apparently.

Harrison continued speaking to her in French and she responded, her eyes going wide, and she gestured with her hands like she was a traffic cop working an intersection. Amazingly she also managed to draw the attention to her lush figure. She was dressed in a pencil skirt and a snug blouse, which framed her assets perfectly, although not in a slutty way. She was sexy but refined. Again, you simply cannot outdress the French.

I caught a smattering of words but not enough to keep up. I tugged his sleeve. He ignored me. I tugged his sleeve again. And he looked at me impatiently.

"What is she saying?" I asked.

"Quite a bit, actually," he said. "She hasn't seen the painting since the court gave it to O'Toole Insurance to be kept in their vault until the court made a ruling on who rightfully owns it. She is stunned about Reyer's death but doesn't see how it could be related to the painting."

"Really, did she say anything about Will?"

"Not yet," he said.

The woman looked at me. She seemed curious and a little wary, which I thought was an interesting reaction.

"You are married?" she asked in English. Her accent was very thick but the question was an easy one.

"Me?" I asked. I gestured between Harry and me. "Us? No, no, just . . . uh . . . er."

"Stop now, before you strain something," he said. He sounded amused. He turned back to Colette. "I'm sorry, how rude of me not to introduce you to my . . . friend. Colette Deneau, this is Scarlett Parker."

"How do you do?" I asked. I didn't really like being his "friend," especially when Colette's eyes lit up just a little, no doubt at the thought that he was available or edible judging by the way she was looking at him. Hmm.

"Do you know anyone who would have wanted to harm

Monsieur Reyer?" I asked. "You know, over a painting, perhaps?"

My accusation was not subtle and she reared back like I'd slapped her.

"I am shocked," she said. Her pretty eyes went wide and then a little watery. "I am so sorry to hear about Mr. Reyer."

This surprised me since it hadn't sounded like she and Mr. Reyer were on the best of terms. My face must have shown as much as she looked at me and nodded.

"It is true we disagreed on the painting," she said. "He felt that it truly was his since he bought it from the *bouquiniste*, but I paid what he asked for it, so . . ."

"Did you know it was a Renoir?" Harrison asked.

"No," she said. "I only hoped that perhaps it was more valuable than ten euros. I was amazed, just amazed, when Mr. O'Toole at the insurance company told me its history."

"Are you hoping that the court decides that the painting belongs to you?" I asked. Since she was being so forthcoming, I figured, what the heck, maybe she would admit that she was furious that the painting had been taken from her and she was looking for revenge. It was a long shot but we had nothing to lose.

"Oh, no," she said. "I truly hope that the painting is given back to the Musée de l'Or. Everyone should be able to enjoy such a beautiful piece. Besides, I heard it was the final request of the original owner, Madame Brouillard. That should be respected."

I admired her generosity of spirit. Although she seemed overly interested in Harrison, Colette Deneau also seemed to be a stand-up gal. She was more interested in everyone getting to appreciate the Renoir than she was the big payout, unlike Jacques Reyer. Perhaps that was why he was dead and she wasn't.

Harrison asked her about the Brouillards and she said she hadn't met them but had heard of them from Mr. O'Toole. She said that they still lived in the family estate and, as far as she knew, hadn't made a formal claim on the painting.

Harrison and I took our leave not really having any more questions for her. I was still rattled that she had asked about our marital status. Did we present ourselves like a married couple? Why did that make me feel all breathless and giddy? I mean, Harrison wasn't even my boyfriend . . . yet . . . how could I entertain thoughts of him as a husband?

Husband! Oh, bother. Because I was so flustered, I forgot to ask Colette whether she knew Will. I wanted to know if he had been in the office when she brought the painting to O'Toole's. I don't know why, but I was holding out some sort of crazy hope that she might have seen something or learned something, maybe from Reyer, or the media, or perhaps even Mr. O'Toole, something that would give us a clue as to who would have grabbed Will and why.

"Hang on," I said to Harry. "I forgot to ask her something."

I ran back up the stairs to Colette's place. I rapped

quickly on the door, not wanting her to get preoccupied with something else and ignore me.

The door swung open and she stood there with a drink in one hand and a cigarette in the other. I could smell the alcohol wafting off the glass as she blew out a plume of smoke that shot right by my face, so not quite the ingénue she had appeared to be.

Chapter 20

"So sorry," I said. "I forgot to ask you if you ever met a man named Will Graham?"

One of her arched eyebrows rose, and she looked at me as if trying to figure out why I would ask her such a question.

"He works for O'Toole Insurance," I said. "He is my cousin's, well, he's a close family friend."

"How close?" she asked. I saw her nostrils flare just a little and I could see that my babbling was not making much sense to her.

"Very close," I said. "Listen, he was grabbed the other night, right after he showed us the painting, a big black car pulled up and he was snatched."

"He showed you and Mr. Wentworth?" she asked.

"No, my cousin, Vivian, and I," I said.

"Vivian?" she asked. She glanced behind me as if looking for someone. "Is she with you?"

"No," I said. "She's teaching a hat-making class at the Paris School of Art over on the Left Bank."

"She is pretty, like you?" she asked.

I actually felt myself blush. There was something intensely flattering about Colette's scrutiny, which also made me nervous. It was like being in middle school when one of the cool kids deigns to talk to you and you're not sure why.

I wondered if Colette did this to men. I'd have to ask Harry. Scratch that, if she did affect Harry, I didn't want to know. My self-esteem didn't need a hit like that.

"Vivian is much lovelier than I'll ever be," I said. "She's quite beautiful, actually."

Her eyes seemed to harden at that like little chips of darkness with no light shining through. The veneer of innocence she'd seemed to have before was gone. Maybe it was the cigarette or the booze, but right now, she looked like a driven woman, the sort who would have no trouble going after what she wanted and knocking down anyone who stood in her way.

"You do not give yourself enough credit," she said. "You are quite lovely and I am sure this cousin of yours cannot be much more so."

Her tone was dismissive, and I sensed she was going to close the door on me. I stalled.

"Okay," I said. I wasn't going to argue. "Are you quite certain you never met Will Graham?" I asked again. There was a note of desperation in my voice that was not faked. Will had been gone for almost forty-eight hours, we hadn't heard from him, and I for one was getting very worried.

She shrugged. She didn't seem to appreciate my anxiety at all. I wondered if that was a French thing or if it was just her. I suspected it was just her as I couldn't imagine Suzette just shrugging at me when I was worried about something.

"Maybe, maybe not," she said. "It was very chaotic once it was discovered that the painting looked to be authentic. I truly can't say if I met him."

We stared at each other for a moment. I got the distinct feeling she knew something that she wasn't telling me. It made me want to pinch her really hard.

"I like the color of your door," I said, trying to get back some sort of rapport. "It's very cheerful."

"*Porte jaune*," she said.

"I'm sorry," I said. "My French is rusty."

"It means yellow door," she said, looking at me as if I was dull-witted. Then she sent me a small smile through another plume of smoke.

I could have stayed and asked her more questions; instead I murmured a civil thank-you and left, not even waiting for her to say "you're welcome" or "good-bye." I had a feeling she wasn't going to offer either sentiment anyway.

Harry was right where I'd left him; he was talking on his phone and frowning. The vee in between his eyes was carved deep and the corners of his mouth were turned down.

"Thanks, mate," he said into the phone. "Call me if you find anything, anything at all."

"Mate?" I asked. "Was that Alistair?"

"It was," he said. "What did you have to dash back up there for?"

"Why did you call Alistair?" I countered.

"I asked first," he said. He took my hand once again and we left the courtyard and wandered back onto the street.

"First? Are we really playing it this way?" I asked.

"Yes," he said.

"Fine," I said. Then I gave him my most wicked grin and dropped my voice a few octaves and gazed at him through my lashes. "I'll show you mine if you show me yours."

Harrison looked as if I'd smacked him up the side of the head with a teapot.

"You can't . . . that's not . . . Ginger," he said. His voice was a slow growl that sounded absolutely delicious. "You're not playing fair."

"All's fair in lo—" I cut myself off with a gasp. Had I almost said it, the "L" word? We weren't ready for that. We hadn't even rounded the bases and slid into home yet. Not even once.

I glanced at him and he was grinning. Of course he was!

"Figure of speech," I said. "Do not read into that."

His grin deepened. For a breathless second I thought he was going to kiss me, and I knew I wouldn't be able to hide my feelings if he did.

"What did you call Alistair for?" I begged in an effort to change the subject.

He was still grinning at me when he answered, "I'm having him run a background check on Colette just to see if she is as she appears."

"She's not," I said. "I went back to ask if she remembered meeting Will, she said she didn't, but—"

"You don't believe her," he said.

"It was hard to get past the glass of booze and cigarette," I said. "She went from young innocence to hardened adult in less than five minutes."

"Interesting," he said.

We continued walking back to the lamppost with the red Metro sign on it.

"Did you let Alistair know that Viv is still in love with her husband?" I asked.

"No," he said.

"Do you think that's wise?" I asked. "He might get crushed."

"I hinted that, with Will missing, Viv's feelings were a bit of a muddle."

"Was he okay with that?"

I really liked Alistair Turner. He was funny, charming, smart, and with his lithe build and chin-length dark hair, he was not hard on the eyes either. Yes, understatement.

Then again, I liked Will, too. He was also funny and charming with his down-home good looks and pleasant disposition. I really didn't envy the situation Viv was in;

however, if we didn't find Will, I guess it wouldn't be so tricky. The thought depressed me.

"He's fine with it," he said. Something in his voice sounded off. I looked at him with my most dubious gaze and he sighed. "All right, fine. I haven't exactly mentioned that Viv is waffling on the whole annulment thing."

"Harry," I cried. "Alistair could get his heart broken."

"No, he won't," he said. "He's a grown lad and it's not as if he and Viv have anything going. She's been shooting him down for months. He'll be fine."

Men. They were positively thick as bricks at times. I began to roll my eyes but then had to abandon it as Harry wasn't looking at me and we were entering the Metro stop and I didn't want to crash into anyone.

"We need to go tell Viv about Jacques Reyer," I said. "I don't want her to hear about it on the news. Also, we should probably get in touch with Inspecteur Lavigne, don't you think?"

"I suppose you're right," he said.

We hurried to the platform, arriving just as the train did. Harry unlatched the door and we climbed aboard. We'd have to take a couple of trains back to the Left Bank, where our apartment and the school were located.

Harry checked the time on his watch and I glanced at him. "Have a hot date?"

"Actually, we both do," he said.

"What do you mean?"

Harrison gave me an enigmatic smile but refused to elaborate, although I badgered him unmercifully all the way home and believe you me, I can badger with the best of them.

* * *

"Scarlett, darling, how are you?" a voice called out from the drawing room as Harrison and I entered the vestibule of the apartment building.

Suzette smiled at us as she closed the door behind us and she and Harrison exchanged a knowing look.

"Is that—" I dashed into the drawing room, and sure enough, sitting by the fire were my two closest friends, Nick Carroll and Andre Eisel.

"Oh, wow, you're here!" I cried. I jumped up and down and held out my arms for a hug. I dropped my arms. "Wait! What are you doing here?"

"We're the cavalry," Nick said. He was wearing a snappy suit and his thinning blond hair was gelled to perfection.

"No, we're not, I don't like horses. They have too many teeth. It freaks me out," Andre Eisel, Nick's partner, said. In a body-hugging gray cashmere sweater and jeans, he looked even more stylish than Nick. With his dark complexion and close-cropped hair, he looked more like a fashion model than the renowned photographer that he was.

"That's what I like about them," Nick protested. "Great choppers." Being a dentist, that is what Nick would like about them.

They ignored my arms at my sides and scooped me close in a group hug. It was a rib cracker and forced the breath from my lungs before they let me go.

"Sit, sit," Suzette said as she came back into the room behind Harrison. "I made tea."

The end of my nose was still cold as well as the tips of my ears. I was very grateful for a cup of black tea with a heaping teaspoonful of sugar.

"I still don't understand," I said. I took off my beret and shrugged out of my coat. "What are you doing here?"

"I sent for them," Harrison said.

"In the company jet, no less," Nick said. "Very posh."

"I like having a friend who's a toff," Andre said.

Harrison shook his head. He knew that the boys were incorrigible. He sat next to me on the sofa and Andre sat on the other side. Suzette and Nick took the two remaining seats in front of the fire.

"Explain," I said to Harry.

"We need help," he answered. "So, I called Nick and Andre to see if they could pop over and help us look for William."

I glanced at my two friends. "You're that curious to get a look at Viv's husband, are you?"

"That's gratitude," Nick said to Andre, giving me a hurt look.

I was not buying it.

"My husband?" Viv asked as she entered the room. "Who saw my husband?"

Her face was so full of hope that I felt just awful and I cringed as I got to my feet and said, "Oh, Viv, no one. I'm sorry, I misspoke."

"Oh." Viv met my gaze and her shoulders dropped in disappointment, making me feel even worse. "Nick, Andre, what are you doing here?"

"We're here to help, love," Andre said. "Harrison brought us in."

"Oh, thank you," Viv said. She sounded a little cheered by the arrival of our friends. "I know we'll find him; I just know it."

They exchanged hugs and Harrison dragged another chair from the side of the room over so that Viv had a seat, too.

"Did anything happen at the school today?" I asked. I had been worried that Emile St. James would show up, or that she would hear about Jacques Reyer before we had a chance to tell her.

"Nothing," she said. "My class is going well. My students have really taken to millinery. They only have two and a half more days to finish their hats for Saturday's fashion show." She turned to Nick and Andre. "You'll be here for it, won't you?"

"Wouldn't miss it," Nick said.

"Absolutely," Andre assured her.

"And hopefully Will is going to be there, too," Viv said.

She looked so forlorn, I felt my chest get tight. Suzette handed her a cup of tea and Viv gave her a small smile of thanks but it didn't light her eyes, and I knew her worry for Will was beginning to grind her down.

"He will be," Andre said. He sounded so confident, as only someone who hadn't been here for the past few days could, that even I almost believed him.

"Here's what we know so far," Harrison said.

He went on to tell the assembled group about the Renoir

and how Will had shown it to Viv and me right before it went missing. He added in Will's encounter with Emile St. James and then our own meeting with him at the cemetery.

"Emile St. James, why does that name sound familiar?" Nick asked. He tapped his chin with his right forefinger. "I know I've heard it before. I just know it."

"He's a miserable bastard," I said. "He's one of those people who is consumed by owning beautiful things, as if it makes him more valuable as a person, which it doesn't."

"I know the type," Andre said. "A few of them have hired me over the years to take pictures of their treasured possessions. It's a scary narcissism that dwells inside of a person who buys, or steals, a piece of art, locking it away in a vault so that only he can ever see it."

"Scary narcissism, yeah, that sounds like St. James," I said.

"Except St. James doesn't have the painting and his method to get it, intimidating Will, didn't work," Harrison said. "And now that Reyer has been murdered—"

"A murder?" Andre asked. "You might have led with that, mate."

"Sorry," Harrison said. "It's been a rather full day."

"Reyer, the shopkeeper? What?" Viv asked. "When? How? Do you think . . . was there any indication . . . about Will?"

Chapter 21

It was painful to watch Viv struggle for words. I knew she had to be terrified and I wished more than anything that I could put her mind at ease.

"We don't know for certain when he was killed, but we found him in his shop this morning," I said. Andre leaned toward me and squeezed my hand with his. Finding a body together was the bond that had cemented our friendship so I knew he understood how distressing this morning had been.

Harrison told the others about finding Reyer, calling the police, playing the tourist bit, and then how we searched his office to find the address of the woman who had bought the painting.

We then shared our impressions of Colette Deneau. I noted that Harry didn't describe her as attractive, although

I certainly would have. I found this to be an endearing quality of his. He really did make me feel as if I was the only girl for him. Man, I hoped he still felt the same way two months from now.

"Scarlett, what was your impression of the woman?" Viv asked.

"Initially, she seemed as cheerful as her yellow front door," I said.

"*Porte jaune*?" Suzette asked. I think I was speaking too fast for her and I glanced at Harry and he nodded that the translation was correct.

"Yes, her front door was painted a very happy shade and she seemed to be as well, until I went back the second time and then she seemed rather surly and grumpy," I said. I made an effort to speak more slowly so that I didn't lose Suzette.

"Why the change in attitude?" Nick asked.

I shrugged. "She insisted she didn't know Will but I got the feeling she was hiding something."

"I have Alistair running a background check on her," Harrison said.

We all looked at Viv, who blushed a pretty shade of pale pink. She cleared her throat and looked at Harry and asked, "How is Alistair?"

"He's fine," he said. There was an awkward silence as everyone in the room glanced between them, waiting for more. "And he would likely strangle me if I didn't tell you what he told me, which is that he misses you."

Viv's faint blush turned fiery hot. She lifted her cup to her lips and I had a feeling she was wishing that the tea was straight whiskey. She averted her gaze so I assumed any discussion of Alistair was closed.

"Right. What's our next move then?" Nick asked.

"We're going to split up," Harrison said. "We need to visit the Brouillard family and the Musée de l'Or as both had an interest in the painting. Since we think the painting is linked to Viv's husband disappearing, I figure if we find the painting, we find the husband."

"Seems reasonable enough," Andre said. "Who gets the museum and who gets the family?"

"I've thought about it and I think the best pairings are Nick and Scarlett at the Brouillard estate, and Andre and I at the museum," Harrison said. "Nick, you can pose as an art collector and inquire about a few of the pieces that the family has offered for sale. Andre and I will go to the museum and talk to the curator in charge of the collection in which the Renoir was supposed to belong. Any questions?"

"If Nick is posing as the art collector," I said, "then who am I?"

"His assistant," Harrison said.

"Um, sexist much?" I asked. I gave him a look that let him know how unhappy I was with that.

"You need to see the bigger picture," he said.

"Ha! That one's good enough to frame, mate," Andre said.

Nick burst out laughing and I frowned. Really? Puns now? Viv seemed lost in thought but Suzette was smiling at the boys' antics.

"Oh, don't get riled, Scarlett, it's the state of the art," Nick said.

Harry and Andre both laughed and my frown deepened.

"This conversation is as exciting as watching paint dry," I said.

All three men went abruptly serious, but Suzette giggled, cementing her place in my heart forever.

"What do you want me to do?" Viv asked.

Suzette and I sobered immediately as we all turned to look at Viv. She looked so forlorn that I instantly felt horrible for making light when she had so much worry weighing upon her.

"You are to keep teaching," Harrison said. "We still don't know what Emile St. James's part is in all of this, but it's a good bet that he's going to be watching you."

She nodded. "I'm the decoy then."

"Exactly," he said. He moved to give her a half hug. "I know this is hard, but it's for the best."

She looked unhappy but accepting.

"Should I do an American accent?" Nick asked. Then he gave an example. "Nick Carroll, rich Hollywood mogul, pleased to meet you."

"Not bad," I said. "But I think you'll have better luck as a snobby Brit."

"Truly?" he asked. "I quite fancied myself as a mogul, or perhaps a Texas oilman. You know 'Howdy, partner' and all that."

Nick's Texas accent was thick enough to spread on toast and I had to press my lips together to keep from laughing.

"No," Andre said. "You'll cock it up by saying 'mate'

or some other such thing. Besides, you'd need a cowboy hat to be a true Texan."

"He's right," I said. "They don't go anywhere without their hats or boots."

Nick looked put out but I glanced past him and noted that Andre looked vastly relieved. I turned my head to hide my smile.

As luck would have it, one of the apartments opened up and Nick, Andre and Harrison rented it from Suzette. On the one hand, I was sorry to have Harrison leave the sofa in our little apartment. On the other hand, it was probably for the best since I was already spending so much time with him, and having finally admitted my feelings for him to myself, being in close proximity with him was straight-up torture.

After a dinner that Nick cooked in their small apartment, Viv went right to bed. I suspected she was going to have a nice cry, but when I listened at her door, I didn't hear anything. Maybe the constant stress and worry had simply tuckered her out. Not to mention, the toll teaching her class was taking—that had to be exhausting as well.

I lingered in the living room while Harrison repacked his bag before heading down to his new place. It occurred to me that with the new teams, me with Nick and him with Andre, I wouldn't be seeing as much of him the next day. Disappointment is a very hollow feeling, isn't it?

"That's sorted then," Harry said as he zipped his bag.

He hefted it off the table and set it on its wheels. "I suppose I'll see you at breakfast so we can finalize our plans."

"All right," I said.

We walked to the door together, as I needed to lock it after he left. I took a moment to study him. His wavy brown hair hung over his forehead, and his bright green eyes studied my face as if he had something on his mind but he didn't know how to say it. I knew exactly how he felt.

I opened the door for him and he dragged his bag out into the hall. He paused and gave me a faint smile.

"Good night, Ginger," he said.

"Good night, Harry," I said. "I . . . I'll miss you tomorrow."

For a second we just stared at each other, and then because I just couldn't resist, I rose up on my toes and planted a kiss on his lips. It was swift but no less potent for its brevity, knocking my internal thermostat up into the red zone. Hoo, baby!

I broke the kiss and stepped back. Harry looked like he'd been sucker punched, pretty close, and I laughed as he shook his head as if he was trying to unscramble his brain.

"I'll miss you, too," he said. For a second, I thought he was going to kiss me again, but he didn't. He took a step back, looking as if it cost him quite a lot to make himself do that. And didn't that just win my heart over even more? Then he waved, and said, "'Til tomorrow then."

"Tomorrow," I said and closed the door, locking it behind him. A sigh whooshed out of me that I swear came all the way up from my feet. I tried to remind myself that the hardest thing to do was generally the right thing to do. It was cold comfort, especially in January in Paris in a big bed all by myself.

"Here's how we'll play it," Nick said. "While Madame Brouillard is showing me the pieces that are for sale, you check out the house, looking for any sign of the Renoir."

"If the Brouillards stole the painting back, do you really think they're going to leave it in plain sight?" I asked.

"Sometimes that's the best hiding spot," Nick said.

"Maybe," I said. But I wasn't convinced.

We were being driven in a luxury car to the Brouillards' estate. They lived in Neuilly Sur Seine, a very wealthy neighborhood northwest of central Paris. Our driver paid no attention to us as we rolled along through the neighborhood, which was filled with enormous estates all belonging to those living much larger lives than the rest of us.

"Nick, what if the Brouillards are the ones who took Will?" I asked. I kept my voice low so that the driver wouldn't hear.

"Well, that's a dark twist, isn't it?" Nick asked. He fidgeted with the sleeves on his jacket, the only outward sign that he was a bit nervous.

Andre had dressed him in a black dress shirt and black suit, shaking his head when Nick had appeared this morning in a purple velvet suit with a silk lime green dress shirt. They had haggled but Andre had won. Thank the fashion gods for that!

Since I was supposed to look like his Girl Friday, I was wearing low-heeled black boots and a slim skirt in dark gray with a white turtleneck sweater. The only thing that livened up the look at all was the wide black belt at my hips.

We pulled into a driveway that had a wrought iron gate, which had been left open. Harrison had someone in his office arrange the meeting and our story was that an investor, Nick, was looking to buy some pieces of art. Because the Brouillards were looking to sell some artwork, it seemed all very coincidental and yet plausible, or so I hoped.

The driver stopped on the circular drive right in front of the house. Three stories of thick cream-colored stone loomed over us. The line of the green mansard roof was broken up by several windows, all of which seemed to be looking down upon us in deep disapproval.

Nick led the way up the wide stone staircase to the front door. It was a massive rectangle of ornately carved wood framed by two half-dead, as in brown and withered, topiary shrubs in pedestal vases, one on each side of it. I wasn't sure if the brown leaves were caused by neglect or the weather, but I suspected the former. Either way, they were not welcoming.

From the road, the house had looked resplendent, but up close it was easy to see that the black shutters on the windows were desperate for fresh paint, there were piles of leaves collected in the corners of the wide veranda, and a window to the right had a large crack in the pane of glass and it looked as if someone had used clear tape to patch it.

I gathered times were tough for the Brouillards, which made sense given that they were willing to sell some of their famed art collection. Nick rang the bell and we waited. In moments the door was opened by a woman who was short and stout and looked to be somewhere in her fifties. She had once been blond but now it appeared that the silver was winning. Her clothes were couture, cut to flatter her larger frame, and were entirely too nice for house staff. Nick must have thought so, too.

"*Bonjour, Madame Brouillard*," he greeted her.

"Mr. Carroll, good day," she said. Her French accent was very soft, as light as whipped butter in a croissant.

"So sorry to disturb you on the staff's day off," Nick said.

The smile she bestowed upon him was tinged with relief. Clearly, she had been dreading trying to explain why she was answering her own door and Nick had solved the problem for her. Well played.

"It is no bother," she said. She glanced at me just over his shoulder.

"My assistant, Fiona Felton," he said. We had already decided that I would use our hat shop intern's name instead of my own on the off chance that she had heard my name in connection with Will or the missing Renoir from the police or another source.

"How do you do, Mademoiselle?" she said.

"Very well, thank you," I said.

She led us into the house. It was much like the outside, beautiful but with a sad air of neglect hanging about it, sort of like a coating of dust on an old antique. The chandelier overhead was dull and sported a few cobwebs, the staircase that wound up the side of the room to the floor above looked chipped and scuffed and was missing several rails.

We entered a drawing room to the left. The antique carpet was threadbare, the curtains faded from the sun, and the furniture looked to have seen better days with worn armrests and gouged wood.

"Would you care to sit, Mr. Carroll?" Mrs. Brouillard asked.

"Oh, brilliant," he said. "And please call me Nick. I feel that we are to become very dear friends."

"You may call me Marie," she said.

I noticed neither of them asked me to call them anything; I was the help after all. I tried to know my place. I pulled out my phone as if I were taking notes on it. Neither of them paid any attention to me. Shocking, I know.

"Now, Marie, I have to tell you that my passion is for the impressionists and I hear you have quite a few that you are looking to . . ." Nick hesitated, trying to find the right words, and then he added, "find homes for."

She flashed him a smile, again looking relieved at his kindness.

"We have many," she said. "My mother, Estelle Brouillard, was the last real collector in the family and the impressionists were her favorite as well."

I perked up at this, knowing that Estelle was the one who had bequeathed the troublesome Renoir to the Musée de l'Or originally. I wondered if Nick would be able to steer the conversation that way.

“Who were her favorites?” Nick asked.

“Manet, Monet, Renoir,” she said. “Gonzales, Buffet, Pissarro, she loved them all, so much so that she nearly caused the financial ruin of the family all for her passionate love of art.”

“I fear it is an obsession to love the works of the greats so much that you need to own them, to make them yours and yours alone,” Nick said. “I know I feel that way and I imagine your mother felt the same.”

I gave him a side eye. He sounded a little daft, as my cousin would say, while I was more partial to cray-cray.

Marie gave him a wide, toothy grin. Her eyes were hazel, blue with brown around the pupil, and they didn’t reflect the smile on her lips, which seemed terrifyingly calculating. That was the first moment I got the feeling that things might not be as they seemed in that perhaps Marie’s interest in Nick was about more than selling him some art. Uh-oh!

Chapter 22

"Yes, you and my mother would understand each other quite well," she said. She tossed her head and her ash-colored bob shifted about her round face as if trying to give her cheekbones. "Come, I will give you the tour and you can see if we have anything that might interest you."

We began the tour on the first floor. Room after room of musty, neglected furniture. I could feel a sneeze lodge itself in my nose, just waiting to let loose. I pinched the bridge of my nose repeatedly, trying to keep it in.

Nick, bless his heart, kept pace with Marie. He played up the part of the rich collector, asking questions, admiring the works of art, and flattering Marie until she lost the pinched expression on her face and was hanging on his every word.

I feared he might be overselling it, as Marie kicked the

giggling and flirting up a notch, clearly not catching on to the fact that Nick was gay. If Andre were here, he'd likely have a fit. I figured it was just as well that Harry had divided us up as he had, and I wondered how the two of them were doing at the museum.

I surreptitiously took a few pictures of the pieces we were looking at, including an ugly little statue in the corner, all the while pretending to be taking notes. I wondered if the pieces Marie was showing us were authentic. It occurred to me that since Harry and Andre were at the museum, I could text them some of the pictures and the curator could tell us what the known status of the pieces were. You know, like was it really in a museum in Germany or Italy, or was it owned privately by, say, the Brouillards?

I'm not sure why but my intuition was telling me not to trust Marie Brouillard. Perhaps it was the alarming amount of teeth she showed when she smiled or maybe it was the fact that she looked at Nick as if she were cataloging the cost of each item of his clothing—again, thank goodness Andre had dressed him today—and was estimating his worth accordingly. Either way, there was something about her I didn't trust.

I fired off a quick text to Harry with some pictures attached. So far, we had seen a number of small pieces by a variety of impressionists. They were pretty cool, but none were the Renoir we were looking for, and they were all modest-sized pieces that didn't really knock my boots off.

There was a gallery on the second floor that was full of art. Most of it, according to Marie, was junk. They were mostly artists who had come up in the Paris art scene who had shown great promise but then didn't become as successful as was speculated.

I had never thought of fine art as a gamble before, but looking at the vast array of paintings in the room that were now worth nothing, I realized thousands of dollars had been spent looking for a sure thing, but in art, unless it was an established artist who was already untouchable, there really wasn't a riskless gamble.

Nick was doing a fine job of playing the art connoisseur. He paced the room, propped his chin on his hand while considering a piece. He asked Marie questions, giving me the opportunity to snap a few more pictures, although there was still no sign of the Renoir, which I was beginning to think was more and more of a long shot. I decided it was time to be a bit more direct.

"Excuse me, Madame Brouillard," I said. I waited until she turned her gaze toward me. "I read in the paper that your family bequeathed a Renoir to the Musée de l'Or, but it was stolen shortly afterwards and that it recently turned up in a junk shop. Do you think you'll be getting that piece back?"

"No, we will not," she said. "The painting was insured by the museum, so when it was stolen, the museum was compensated for it. I imagine the painting will belong to the insurance company now."

"Did you ever have any dealings with the insurance company?" I asked.

"No," she said. "There was no need. The painting was no longer ours. My mother fancied herself a patron of the arts, but she was really a poseur, trying to ingratiate herself into the art world by having her name on a plaque beside a painting no one cared about in a smaller museum because she couldn't afford to be a patron in a larger venue."

The bitterness in her tone was as corrosive as acid, and I noted that Nick was watching her with undisguised horror. I had to keep her attention for a moment longer, so he could get back into character.

"Ah," I said. "Have you considered buying it back, maybe talking to someone at O'Toole Insurance about it?"

She gave me a sour look. "No, I do not love art the way my mother did. I would be most happy to have bare walls." She then turned toward Nick and her face broke into a charming smile that was so insincere, at least to me, that it made my skin crawl. "So it is wonderful that Nick is here to relieve me of my burden."

"Quite right," Nick said. "Shall we continue our tour?"

"*Absolument*," Marie said. Her voice was husky. "The next stop is my boudoir."

As she dragged him from the room, Nick threw me a terrified look over his shoulder. I would have laughed out loud but my phone chimed, alerting me that I had a text back from Harrison.

> The statue is another item that was bequeathed by the Brouillard family to the museum and then went missing. Get out of there. Now.

I read the text twice before it sank in. Then I dashed after Nick.

"Mr. Carroll," I cried. "I am so sorry, but we have an urgent business matter to take care of . . ." I paused. I felt that the lie would only take if I could come up with a solid reason, so I added, "It's about the beekeeper on the Carroll estate in Kent."

Nick and Marie were just up ahead of me in the hallway, and my boots made random taps on the floor when I stepped where the carpet was bare and my heels clacked on the wood floor beneath.

Marie raised one eyebrow, looking like she didn't believe me. I guess it takes a liar to know a liar. Nick, on the other hand, looked like he wanted to throw himself in my arms like a toddler needing a hug.

"The apiarist?" he asked, jumping into my lie with Nick-style gusto, probably fueled by relief. "What sort of trouble is he having?" He leaned toward Marie and said as an aside, "Big money in honey these days."

She blinked, and when she looked back at me, I nodded and shrugged.

"Something about a dead queen," I said. "He's requesting a video chat immediately."

Nick frowned in concern and then turned and kissed the back of Marie's hand, the very picture of one aristocrat schmoozing another. She put her hand to her throat and tittered with pleasure. I tried not to roll my eyes.

"Madame," I said. "One of the pieces we would be interested in is that statue in the drawing room. Is it an original?"

Marie stared at me for a moment. A hint of red crept up her neck, but her gaze never wavered. "It is a copy, I'm afraid. My mother bequeathed the original to the museum, but she loved it so much that she had a copy made. She did that with several of her most precious pieces."

"Oh, bad luck," Nick said. "Still, you have a lovely collection. Is it all right if I call upon you again?" He lowered his voice and added, "I feel we have unfinished business."

"It would be my pleasure," Marie said. She looked like she wanted to take a bite out of him. *Ew!*

She walked us to the door and watched as our driver let us into the car. As soon as the driver closed the door behind us, Nick collapsed against the seat.

"Serve me between two slices of bread and call me a sandwich," he said. "That woman was terrifying."

"You handled her very well, you manly man, you," I said.

Nick tossed his thinning blond hair in a look of male pride. "I'm irresistible, it's a curse."

I laughed and then opened my phone to call Harrison and tell him we were on our way back to the apartment.

"Good," he said. He sounded edgy.

"Are you all right?" I asked. He made a grumbling sound, which didn't really answer my question so I forged on. "Listen, I asked Marie Brouillard about the statue—"

"Ginger, what were you thinking?" he interrupted. "If she's involved with the art theft—"

"She's not," I interrupted. "Believe me, she was more interested in putting the moves on Nick."

"Oh."

"Yeah."

"Oy. I'll feel better when I have you in sight," he said.

"There's something very dodgy about the entire situation. The curator at the museum studied the picture you sent of the statue and she is quite sure that it is the original, so why does Marie Brouillard have a statue that she thinks is a copy?"

"How can the curator be sure?" I asked.

"A subtle marking on the base, not something that would have been replicated by someone making a copy," he said.

"If Marie has the original, then . . ." My voice trailed off and Nick studied me with his eyebrows raised.

"Then it's safe to assume that someone is running a fraud," Harrison said. "Possibly Marie or someone associated with the Brouillards."

"You mean you think that Estelle Brouillard bequeathed items to museums but then her family stole them back?" I asked.

"Quite possibly," he said. "And if Will got wind of it . . ."

"She may have killed him or had him killed to keep the secret," I said.

"Marie Brouillard, a murderess?" Nick asked. His normal pink complexion went white and waxy.

"We're going to need proof," I said.

"We'll get it," Harry said. "Just get home. I have a deep-seated need to hug you."

I heard Andre make retching noises in the background and I laughed. "One bear hug coming up."

"Harrison gets a bear hug?" Nick asked, outraged. "I'm the one who put my life on the line, posing as a straight man. Why does he get a hug?"

"Oh, poor Nick," I said. I tucked my phone back into my purse and wrapped my arms about him and gave him a crusher hug. He put his head on my shoulder and sighed.

"Better?" I asked.

"A little," he said.

"Did the scary old lady frighten you?" I asked.

"Yes," he said. "But even worse, that house gave me the collywobbles. Did you see what a mess it was? Servants' day off, my arse."

When we arrived back at the apartment building, it was midafternoon. Andre had insisted on stopping at a patisserie on their way back from the museum, and he and Harrison had brought all the fixings for a sweet tea.

Suzette let Nick and Andre use her kitchen to make tea. Although it was a clear day outside, the sun could not heat the chill temperature of the air, and since the Brouillard house had been chilly, I felt it all the way into my bones.

Not being much good in the kitchen, I stayed in the drawing room by the fire, looking at the pictures I had managed to take while in the Brouillard estate. I was pretty impressed with myself as I had snapped more than I thought. I figured we could send them to the curator at the museum that Harry had spoken with and see if she knew if any others had been donated and then gone missing.

It was here that Harrison found me when he returned from his room. He had gone up to change out of the stuffy suit he'd been wearing and was now looking quite dishy, as Viv would say, in a pair of well-worn jeans and a thick wool sweater in a deep shade of forest green.

"Ginger," he said. He came straight toward me with

purpose in his every step. He didn't stop but scooped me up and into his arms and held me tight.

I wrapped my arms about his shoulders and hugged him in return, mostly so that I could absorb his warmth. And boy howdy, did I. All of a sudden, I wasn't just warm, I was overheating.

If this were a romance novel, this would be the moment when he kissed me and begged me to go out with him, my ban on dating be damned. But he didn't. Harrison was above all else a good guy and he wouldn't have me renege on my promise to myself because he supported me in all that I did. Damn it.

Instead, we stood in front of the fire with our arms around each other. Neither of us spoke, not wanting to break the spell of being fireside in Paris with the person of our heart. Okay, so that was why I wasn't saying anything. I could only hope that Harry felt the same. Frankly, if he didn't, I didn't want to know.

"All right, you two, chaperones are in the room, break it up," Andre said as he entered the room bearing a heavily loaded tray with Nick right behind him carrying a fully loaded tray of his own. Suzette followed, carrying a stack of plates, and closed the door behind her.

It was with great reluctance that I let go of Harry. I examined the tea tray the boys brought in. Well, I supposed if I had to console myself with a morsel or two from the patisserie, so be it. I picked a *chou à la crème*, puff pastry with cream, because if that can't fix what ails you, nothing can.

Harry poured me a cup of tea and I sat down and nibbled

on my cream puff. I let Nick do the talking and he told them all about Marie Brouillard and the estate that was falling down. In turn, Andre caught us up to speed on what the curator at the Musée de l'Or had to say. It appeared that several of the items that Estelle Brouillard had bequeathed to the museum had recently reappeared on the black market after the insurance company had paid out to the museum.

There was a knock on the drawing room door, and Suzette rose to answer it. I took a sip of my tea and then looked at Harrison. The coincidence was too much to ignore.

"Do you think it's a scam then?" I asked. "I mean, it must be, right?"

He shrugged. "It's possible."

"If it is an insurance scam, then that means that Will probably caught wind of it, and Marie Brouillard had him kidnapped to keep him from interfering. If she's that ruthless, she may even have had him killed."

A strangled cry sounded, and I glanced at the door to see Viv standing there, with her hand at her throat, looking horror-struck.

Chapter 23

"Oh, Viv, I'm sorry," I cried. This was the second time I'd blasted her with bad news when she walked into the room. When would I learn to think before I spoke? "That was thoughtless of me to say; it was mere speculation, just hypothetical, not fact. Pastry?"

I held up my plate, hoping she would join me in the restorative powers of a tarte or a bright-colored macaron, but she shook her head, waving me off.

"You think Will is dead? Why?" she cried.

Andre and Nick stood and began fussing over her like mother hens, taking her coat and handing her a cup of tea. Once she was settled, they resumed their seats as well.

We took turns telling her everything. When she looked like she might cry, Suzette put a comforting arm around her and Viv leaned into her. Although she was closer to our age than our mothers', there was something about Suzette that was very motherly. It was one of the many things about her that I liked.

The buzzer from the street sounded and Suzette rose to go answer the door.

"I'd best go with you," Harrison said. "For safety's sake."

He put down his tea and followed her from the room. I wondered if this was how cautious we would need to be until we discovered what had happened to Will.

"It's going to be all right, Viv," I said. I moved and took the spot beside her on the couch. "We're figuring some things out, but we will find Will, I promise."

I felt as if I'd made this promise several times already and I wondered if Viv was losing her faith in me and the rest of us.

"Is this what you lot consider hard work?"

I glanced up at the door and in strode Alistair Turner. He looked as dashing as ever with his dark chin-length curls, arching eyebrows, square jaw and sharp-edged cheekbones.

"Alistair, mate, what are you doing here?" Nick asked.

Both he and Andre rose to shake hands and slap our friend on the back. I gave him a quick hug and Viv gave him a tiny wave and a flash of a smile. Judging by the way he stared at her, as if the wind had been knocked out of him, the wave was more than enough.

"Alistair, you didn't have to come all this way," Viv said.

"Oh, but I did." He turned toward Harrison and Suzette as they entered the room behind him. "I have news."

"Good, I hope," Harrison said. "We could use some."

"The woman you had me track down, Colette Deneau, I found a warrant for her arrest in Belgium for fraud, and get this, her real name is Colette Brouillard Deneau."

Harry and I exchanged matching looks of shock. I sat down hard on the sofa. The rest of the group followed suit, with Suzette dashing off to make more tea.

"Do you know what this means?" I asked.

"No, remind me who Colette is again?" Nick asked.

"She's the woman who bought the painting from Jacques Reyer and brought it to O'Toole's to have it appraised," Harrison said.

"But she's a Brouillard," Andre said. "Which could be coincidence—"

"It's not," Alistair said.

"Which means she's related to Marie Brouillard, I'm guessing her daughter or maybe a niece, judging by the difference in their ages," I said. "So this is just one huge scam that they are running."

"How do you figure?" Viv asked.

I put my pastry down, that alone tells you how stressed I was, and began to pace around the room as I worked out the details in my theory.

"Emile St. James is hot to own that painting," I said. "He can't be the only one. Given the condition of the Brouillard estate, they are on the verge of losing everything."

"They are," Harrison said. "I ran their financials, and

it looks like the estate will be declared bankrupt in a matter of weeks."

"So, they need money and fast," I said. "The curator said that several of the pieces that I sent you pictures of had been stolen from the museum over the years, which means the whole thing is just a way to make money for the Brouillards."

"How?" Nick asked. He looked baffled.

"They must donate the art to a museum, get a tax write-off, then steal the art back. We'll have to ask Colette how they manage that trick. Then they likely plant the painting or what have you somewhere, say a *bouquiniste* or boutique, and buy it back for nothing, making its origin unknown. Then they can sell it on the black market to people like Emile St. James, in a payout Will told us could be well into six or possibly seven figures."

"It didn't exactly work out that way this time, did it?" Andre asked.

"No," I said. "I'm thinking the trouble with the Renoir was that Jacques Reyer bought it from the *bouquiniste* first, forcing Colette to buy it from him, which a buyer might have found suspicious. Likely she had to bring it to O'Toole to reassure whoever was looking to buy it that it was authentic and didn't realize that O'Toole had already paid out a policy on that very painting years ago."

Harrison nodded. "Sounds plausible so far."

"When Reyer found out the real value of the piece, he wouldn't let it go and went to the media to plead his case for the painting to be returned to him. That brought so much attention to the piece that Will's company came forward and claimed it, leaving Colette and Marie without the painting, probably getting them in hot water with Emile. Will must have figured out the scam and Colette and Marie hired some thugs to take him away and steal back the painting."

They were all silent, staring at me as if I was mental.

"What?" I asked. "I think I'm on to something here."

Harry nodded. "I agree. The problem is we have to prove it, all of it, to Inspecteur Lavigne before he'll take us seriously."

"I think I can help with that," Alistair said. "I can pose as an art buyer, looking for the Renoir."

"I thought that was my role," Nick said.

"No, your part was to get us into the house," I said. "The way Marie latched on to you, I think you'd be wise to give that one a wide berth."

"Latched on to you, did she?" Andre asked his partner.

Nick shrugged. "Even criminals have taste."

"Clearly," Andre said. He gave his partner an affectionate smile.

"Alistair, you don't have to do this," Viv said.

She sounded timid, so unlike my Viv that we all turned to look at her. Her cheeks were flushed with color, and she was looking at the top of the table, instead of making eye contact with anyone.

"No, I don't," he agreed. She glanced up at him in surprise and he met her gaze and held it. "But I want to. I want to help you."

"I'm married," she said. "That hasn't changed."

"I know," he said. His voice was quiet and soft like he was trying to coax a kitten out of a tree.

It was painful to watch them, and I glanced away, noticing that the others did, too. Well, except for Nick. He was watching with rapt attention like it was a cliff-hanger season ender on *Downton Abbey.* I gave him a quick kick to the ankle.

"Ouch! Oy, Scarlett, that hurt," he said.

"Sorry," I muttered. Then I gave him my intense stare so he'd know why I had tapped him, yes, it was just a tap, with my boot.

Suzette came back into the room with more tea and we all turned our attention to her. Alistair wasn't finished with Viv, however.

"Listen, Viv, I know you're spoken for," he said. "But I also know that I've never felt for anyone the way I feel about you, so I will help you now, and when we get your husband back, if you choose him instead of me, that's all right, because all I truly want is to see you smile again."

Silent tears coursed down Viv's cheeks, and Suzette put the teapot down and put her hand over her heart.

"*Comme c'est romantique*," she said.

I only got the last word, but I totally agreed.

I glanced over at Nick and Andre. Andre looked watery; Nick had given up and had tears coursing down his cheeks. I glanced at Harry and saw him watching me, probably looking to see how I reacted. I gave him a wobbly smile and he nodded. We both liked Alistair very much, but Viv had to follow her heart and I knew we both supported her in that.

"All right, before we all get soggy and useless, let's figure out how we can make this happen," I said.

"Lucas, eh, Mr. Martin, can help," Suzette said. "He invited me to the opening of an art installation at the Musée Rouge. Anyone who is anyone in the art world will be there."

"Most likely including Emile St. James and the Brouillard women," Harrison said. "Great, how do we get in?"

"This was not really what I had in mind when I agreed to go undercover," Nick said. "I definitely had something much more Double-O-Seven in mind."

"No complaining now," Andre said as he straightened Nick's bow tie. "People never see the help; we'll be able to eavesdrop much more effectively disguised as waiters."

Nick heaved a beleaguered sigh.

"And if you see Mrs. Brouillard, avoid her at all costs," I said. "If she recognizes you, the whole thing could blow up in our faces."

"Right. Ready, gang?" Harrison asked. He was our leader as he spoke French the best and could give us our assignments from our boss.

"We're on canapé duty," Harrison said. "So heft your tray and go mingle. Remember, you're listening for any mention of Will's name particularly from either of the Brouillard women or St. James. Keep an eye on who they speak with, and if you can manage it, take a picture so we can try and identify some of the players."

Nick and Andre gave a nod and shouldered their trays, marching out into the crowd like good little soldiers.

"Thanks," I said to Harry before we left the kitchen.

"We couldn't do this without you, and I'm pretty sure it's above and beyond anything in your job description as our business manager."

"I'm not doing it for the job," he said. The look he gave me scorched and it was a good thing we were in the kitchen and near a fire extinguisher because I was pretty sure I was about to go up in flames.

"Ginger—" he began but the event planner interrupted.

A stream of verbally abusive French came out of her mouth as she shouted at Harrison and me.

"Okay, good talk," Harrison said. He jerked his head at the door and we both grabbed our trays and trooped out into the massive gallery.

The space was huge but then it would have to be. The canvases that this artist painted on were massive, ten feet high and twice as wide. Sadly, they weren't really to my taste.

It was a female artist, known only as Canelo. Her preoccupation with the female form came out in her work, or at least that's what I figured, given that the very first piece I saw was a giant boob. No lie, I was nose to nipple with a breast the size of a midsize car.

"Wow," I said. I had to hit the brakes to avoid slamming into Harrison, Nick and Andre, who stood all in a line, staring at the ta-ta like it had an immobility ray shooting out of it.

"Guys! It's just a girl part," I said. "Two of you don't even like girl parts. Snap out of it."

"Sorry, love," Nick said. "It's just that suddenly I have the strongest urge for a glass of milk."

Harrison snorted and I wagged a finger at him and said, "Don't. Don't do it."

"I can't help it, it's a titillating piece," he said.

Andre guffawed, and I frowned at him.

"Stop it," I said. "Focus on our purpose."

"You're right. Sorry, it's just truly the breast painting I've ever seen," Andre said. The others snickered.

"I am leaving you here, idiots," I said. I lifted my tray and started to walk, hissing over my shoulder, "Get moving or this whole event will be a big bust."

They blinked at me and then the three of them started laughing. Oh. My. God. The one time I wasn't even trying to keep up with the word play, and I score the winner. Figures.

I left the boys and worked my way through the crowd, keeping an eye out for Marie Brouillard and Emile St. James.

I saw Suzette, looking lovely in a ruby-colored fit-and-flare cocktail dress, holding Lucas's arm as they moved about the room with Viv and Alistair following them. Lucas, too, looked very handsome in a charcoal gray suit with a black dress shirt, both of which made the silver in his hair look distinguished instead of old.

It had been decided that it would make sense for Viv to be with Lucas and Suzette since she was teaching at the school and living at Suzette's. Meanwhile Lucas was introducing Alistair as an old friend from London who was interested in buying very high-priced pieces of art with the subtle mention that he didn't particularly care if they were aboveboard or not.

Alistair leaned close to Viv and said something while they stood in front of a piece that was clearly a butt cheek. I wondered if they were making puns or if that sort of behavior was left to my immature crew. Judging by the way Viv blushed at his words, I had a feeling they were completely unaware of the big behind looming over them.

Alistair looked amazing as always, in a black suit with a crisp white dress shirt beneath it, no tie. His dark hair contrasted brilliantly against Viv's pale blond curls, and in her form-fitting heather gray sweater dress, which was cut low in the front and the back, they looked like the most glamorous couple in the room.

Except they weren't a couple. I found that bothersome. As much as I liked Will, Alistair was more devoted to Viv's happiness. I couldn't see Alistair marrying Viv on a whim and then disappearing back to his work when she ditched him. No, Alistair was the sort who showed up and fought it out, never giving in until all hope was lost. I liked that about him.

For a moment, I almost went over to check in with them, but then I thought better of it. If this was the last night that Alistair got to have Viv by his side, I was not going to ruin it for the poor guy.

I circled the room, passing Harry once, Andre twice, and never seeing Nick at all. When my tray was empty, I worked my way, the long way, around the room to get back to the kitchen. Smatterings of conversation buzzed in my ears but I didn't see or hear anything of note. I hoped the others were more successful than I was; otherwise this plan really would be a waste. I saw another boob picture out of the corner of my eye. Oh, brother.

Near the kitchen, I noted there was a door half open, leading to another part of the gallery. I wondered if the party had expanded, and if so, were any of the caterers working that room?

I pushed the door wide just to see and then I gasped. Marie Brouillard was in deep conversation with Emile St. James. This was it! This was what we'd been waiting for. I had to hear what was being said. I needed a picture. I dug my hand into my pocket to retrieve my phone. I noticed my hands were shaking from the adrenaline surge that hit me like a punch to the back of the head. Oh, wait, that really was a punch to the head.

The last thing I saw was the floor rushing up to meet me.

Chapter 24

I woke up with a pounder of a headache. A dull throb at the base of my skull mixed in with jolts of pain coming from my temples. It took me a second to realize I was facedown on an upholstered couch. Not the one in our apartment in Suzette's building, no, this was scratchier and lumpier.

It was bright in the room and I blinked. It hurt my eyeballs to have all that light shining in my direction. I kept blinking, trying to block some of the light as I got used to it.

The smell of cigarette smoke curled my nose hair. I pushed off the couch even though it made my head hurt that much more.

Colette was sitting in a nearby chair. She had her hair

teased up on top of her head. She stubbed out her cigarette when she saw me rise and I wondered if she'd lit it specifically to wake me.

"What do you want with me?" I asked. I was going for the age-old play-dumb trick. It had worked before.

"You were looking for me, yes?" she said. "I thought I'd make it easy."

"Why would I be looking for you?" I asked. I tried to make it sound ridiculous with the hope that perhaps she'd let me go if she thought I knew nothing.

"Don't be coy," she said. "You know why."

"No, I really don't," I said. Because I can be stubborn like that.

"Suit yourself," she said. She rose from her seat and left the room. I heard a latch lock the door after her. Rats!

I glanced around the room, looking for a weapon, an escape hatch, an excuse, anything to get me out of here. Art canvases were stacked up against the wall in one corner while sealed boxes had been shoved all along the wall. Were all of these items stolen? I had once read that art museums typically only display about five percent of the art they own. That left an awful lot of work to be stuffed in storage, warehouses, attics, vaults and who knew where else with no one the wiser if the pieces were stolen since the paintings rarely saw the light of day anyway.

I suspected that was what Colette and Marie banked on, literally. I reached into my pocket, hoping that by some small miracle my phone would be there. No such luck. I wondered how long I'd have to wait until Colette came back, and then I wondered if I should punch her in the eye. It seemed as good a place as any.

The door opened and I braced myself, thinking I'd launch myself at her and start swinging, the element of surprise and all. As the door was flung wide, I jumped up and began windmilling my fists, hoping to catch her on the chin or the temple and knock her out.

My plan was partially successful. I clipped the person who entered and he let out a grunt before ducking to avoid my next blow, which was when I recognized him.

"Will? Will, is that you?" I cried. I dropped my fists.

"Scarlett," he said, rubbing his jaw. "Nice punch."

"I'm sorry," I said. "I didn't know it was you. Thank goodness you're here. We've all been looking for you. Are you all right?"

I stepped close to give him a hug. I was so relieved to see him. Viv was going to be so happy to know that her husband was alive. He didn't hug me back. In fact, he held me back with the business end of a very large knife.

"What's going on?" I asked. The sinking feeling in my stomach was sending up flares of the truth, that Will was involved in all this, but I didn't want to acknowledge it. Not yet.

His eyes, which had always seemed so kind before, were flat and cold.

"How did you know I was here?" I asked. "How do you know Colette?"

As if my words had conjured her, Colette appeared in the doorway, looking terrifying with her sly smile. She tossed her phone onto the table by the door and stalked Will, pushing him up against the door frame. I was about to warn him away, but then I noticed he was smiling at her as if she was his best girl. What the what?

She launched herself at him, and he caught her. She wrapped her legs around his waist and he clutched her to him. Then they kissed in a clash of mouths and tongues that would have been more appropriate in a porno film. Not here. Not in front of me. I felt vomit creep up the back of my throat.

It all came into focus now, and it took me out at the knees. Will was in on it, all of it; Will and Colette were two sides of the same evil coin. Colette had the Brouillard family connection and he had the influence in the world of fine art insurance. As far as I could tell, they were a match made in criminal heaven.

Poor Viv, this was a nightmare. While the gruesome twosome were engrossed in each other in a show that I was certain was meant for me, I figured I had two choices—get to the door and run for it, or use the phone Colette had just dropped on the table and call for help.

I went for the phone. I snatched it and turned my back on them as if I just couldn't bear to watch. The phone didn't require a passcode, thank God, so she must have just used it and didn't shut it off. I quickly went to the message icon and opened it. I tapped in Harrison's number.

"Oh, my God," I cried over my shoulder, trying to make them think that I was sickened by their public display of *ew*, not a lie. "I feel ill."

I typed two words—"yellow door"—to Harrison, hoping he would get the message and know that it was from me, and I hit Send. When I turned around, keeping the phone behind my back, Will was staring at me. How had I ever thought he was nice or kind when the look he sent me was so full of contempt and dislike, clearly he thought me the dull-witted sap he had played me for.

"So, Scarlett, meet the wife," he said. Colette disentangled herself from him and then used her thumb to wipe the smear of her red lipstick off his mouth.

"You two are married?" I asked. Okay, that was a surprise.

"Seven years now," Will confirmed. "We met here in Paris in art school."

"Seven years? So, Viv . . . you're not . . ." Shock made me stutter.

"Me married to a hat maker? Hell, no," Will said. He glanced at his wife with lust in his eyes. "I need a woman who is a bit more interesting than that."

"But you slept with her!" I cried. I looked at Colette. This did not appear to be news to her. "Doesn't that mean anything?"

"We do what we must," Colette said. She gave a shrug and I got the feeling they shared an open relationship. Oh, horror!

"Why?" I asked. I looked at Will. "Why use Viv like that?"

"I needed her to get some stolen artwork across the Scottish border for me," he said. "She was so eager to run away and get married, I obliged. Pathetic, really."

"So, that's why you never came after her," I said. "The marriage was a fraud and you didn't love her at all."

He shrugged as if Viv's feelings were less than nothing to him. My heart knotted up in my chest like a fist. This son of a bitch had played on my cousin's grief and used her as little more than a getaway driver. I wanted to hurt him, really, really badly.

I looked at Colette, who was draped around her man like a scarf. Gag. "What does your mother think about all this?"

"My mother?" she asked. She looked confused.

"Marie Brouillard," I said. "She is your accomplice, Colette *Brouillard* Deneau, right?"

Colette looked at Will and then she laughed, long and loud, sort of like a donkey braying in a pasture.

"I told you it would work," she said to him. At my confused look, she added, "I'm not a Brouillard. I used to work for them as a maid, back when they could afford domestic staff. I was also an art student. While working at the Brouillards', I discovered that many of the paintings that had been bequeathed by Estelle were still in the family home.

"Marie insisted they were copies but I had Will authenticate a few of them, and that's when I knew. Estelle had been quite the naughty art patron. She had obviously hired someone to steal the paintings back from the museum and then told her family she'd had copies made. There is a fortune in art in the Brouillard estate, so I helped myself to a few of the pieces. I knew if I posed as a Brouillard, I would be able to sell them for a much higher price."

"And you were a part of this?" I asked Will.

"I had some debt. My dream of being an artist had died.

Colette was working for the Brouillards and convinced me to sell just one piece to start," he said. "We netted a sweet three million off a small Monet. Life was good."

"But expensive," Colette said with a pout. "So we knew we needed to do it again."

"My job with the insurance company helped me connect with the players on the black market," Will said. "And Colette got the idea to create a new identity as Colette Brouillard Deneau, giving us some cred. The Renoir was to be our big score before we retire to Belize."

Criminals. These two were hardened criminals. I knew with a certainty that whatever they had in mind for me, it was not good. The phone in my hand was heavy. I knew I had to get rid of it before Colette noticed it was missing from the table. Still, I had to keep them talking.

"But the Renoir didn't go as expected," I said. "First Jacques Reyer messed it up by buying it from the *bouquiniste* before you could, and then when he found out the value, he refused to let go of his claim on it. Is that why you killed him?"

My heart was in my throat, making my voice tight, and I was having a hard time breathing.

"Scarlett, I'm shocked," Will said. "Do you really think I could kill a man over something like a painting?"

I studied him. He looked like pure evil and my skin crawled. My voice was little more than a whisper. "Yes, I do."

"Well, you're wrong," he said. He grabbed Colette and kissed her. "This little spitfire is the one who clobbered Reyer with the statue, didn't you, lover?"

Again, gag.

Colette was looking at Will as if she was a little bit afraid of him and as if she worshiped him. It was disturbing. It was then that I knew who was the leader and who was the follower. Will was in charge of all of this. That's why Colette killed Reyer, likely because Will told her to.

"Yes, I did," Colette said. She turned to look at me with the craziest eyes I had ever seen. "And I'll kill you, too."

Now I was shaking.

"Now, now, lover," Will said. His voice was soothing as he planted a kiss on her temple. "We need her, at least for the moment."

Colette pouted and then grabbed him by the shirt and kissed him. As they were engrossed in their make-out session, I took the opportunity to drop the phone back onto the little table, and what the hell, I decided to make a run for it.

Chapter 25

I got halfway out the door before Colette landed on my back, taking me to the floor. My knees and hands hit hard, and I yelped. She grabbed me by the back of my hair and pulled me up to my feet, delivering a solid knee to my thigh and making my leg go numb.

"Try that again," she hissed in my ear, "and next time I'll cut you."

She held the big knife Will had been holding up in front of my eyes lest I doubt her sincerity. Okay, then.

"Don't be stupid, Scarlett," Will said. "There is no escape for you."

I wanted to spit in his face, but I realized that might be considered stupid. I yanked my hair out of Colette's hands. *Ouch!* The satisfaction of forcing her to let go was worth the pain that made my eyes water.

Colette looked like she was going to grab me again, but Will held her off.

"Stop. We don't have time for this," he said. "We have to leave for our meeting with St. James."

"Fine," she snapped.

Colette's French accent was thicker with her temper. She narrowed her eyes at me in a look of utter loathing, then she tipped her head to the side and smiled. It was a vicious, cruel smile, the sort that said she knew something that I didn't. It made me afraid, very, very afraid.

She turned her back to me and left the room. Meanwhile Will grabbed my arm and pulled me toward the door. I dug in my heels. Every instinct inside me was screaming that if I went with them, I was dead. I grabbed the door frame with my free hand, and it stopped us, but Will yanked on my other arm, putting all of his weight behind it.

"Wait!" I cried. "Where are you taking me? If the two of you are leaving, why can't you just let me go?"

"Sorry, Scarlett," he said. He didn't look sorry at all. "But we need you."

"What for?" I hated that my voice came out wobbly and nervous. I coughed as if it was phlegm that made me sound weak and not terror.

"We need you to be found stealing the Renoir so that we can disappear," he said. "At first, I thought I'd use Viv for this. I liked the idea of being a widower even if our marriage was bogus, but you'll do just as well. It kind of fits since it's your presence in Paris looking for Viv's husband that has caused me so many problems as it is."

Colette joined us in the foyer. She was holding the

Renoir, the same one that Will had shown me at the insurance office.

"Just think, when they find your body clutching the Renoir to your dead chest, we'll be free," Colette cried. Then she kissed Will on the mouth.

Suddenly, I was dizzy and everything went gray. They were going to kill me. I knew my life was of little to no value to them but surely the painting mattered.

"But the Renoir is worth a fortune," I protested. "You're just going to let it go?"

"Please," Will said. "It's a forgery, a very good forgery by my beloved, but still worthless."

"*Merci, cher,*" Colette said. She simpered and I was torn between passing out, throwing up and slapping her.

Will pried my hand off the door frame and pinned my arms behind my back. "Let's go."

As we exited the apartment, I opened my mouth to yell. Will was one step ahead of me and shoved a handkerchief into my mouth, gagging me.

"Should we shove her in front of a bus or a train?" Colette asked.

My skin felt cold, my teeth would have chattered, but they were blocked by the disgusting cloth in my mouth.

"I'm thinking a roundabout in the Eiffel area," Will said. "All those tourists will make it a nice, splashy news tidbit. That should do nicely."

We trudged down the stairs, well, they trudged and I was dragged, across the small courtyard, toward a waiting car. My eyes scanned the area, hoping against hope that Harrison had gotten my message. There was no one. For a city with over two million people in it, I'd have thought there'd be someone about, but no.

Colette opened the back door of the car and slid in with the forged painting. I noted she still held the knife right where I could see it. Will put a hand on my head and shoved me in after her. I half fell onto the backseat. With my hands free, I yanked the gag out of my mouth and spun around, planning to stop Will from shutting the door, to heck with Colette and her knife. If they were going to kill me anyway, I was going down fighting.

Thwack!

I never got the chance. As I watched, Will slumped to the ground as if someone had let the air out of him. I glanced past him and saw Viv, standing there with a broken bottle of wine in her hand.

"You!" Colette screeched. She dropped the painting, opened her door and dashed out of the car, right into Harrison's arms. He slammed her wrist on the back of the car, forcing her to drop the knife. He quickly subdued her with the help of Nick and Andre, who had moved in right behind him.

Colette bucked and thrashed but she was no match for the three of them. I saw Nick take off his tie and they used it to bind her hands together. Excellent.

I climbed over Will's body to get to Viv. Alistair took the broken bottle out of her hand and kneeled down to check on Will.

"He's got a right knot on his head, but he's breathing. Pity," he said.

Viv opened her arms and I tripped into them. We hugged each other, crying tears of fright and relief, mostly relief.

"Oh, Scarlett," she said. "I was bloody terrified when I realized that you were missing and then Harrison got your text—" She broke off to sob.

Alistair gave us both a quick hug and then took out his phone and said, "I'm calling the police. I'll be right over there."

"What a mangy git," Andre said as he joined us. He nudged Will with the toe of his shoe.

"How did you figure it out?" I asked.

"Harrison got your text and we raced over here," Nick said. "We arrived just in time to see William, the lying sack of sh—"

"We saw him force you down the stairs," Viv interrupted. She cleared her throat as if the next words stuck a bit but she was going to force them out regardless. "And it was clear to see that he and Colette were working together."

"Nick, Andre, a hand here?" Harrison asked.

They each gave me a quick hug and hurried over to Harry.

"Take her back upstairs and keep her there until the police come." He turned Colette over to Nick and then paused beside Viv and me and simply looked at me.

"Yellow door. My clever girl," he said.

Then he cupped my face and kissed me. It was the gentlest kiss, filled with such tenderness as if he was afraid to cause me any more trauma. I could feel a slight tremor in his fingers as he broke the kiss and pressed his forehead to mine.

"I am so very happy to see you, Ginger. You scared me half to death with that text, but thank goodness you did."

"I knew you'd figure it out, my brave boy," I said.

I hugged him really hard and he huffed out a breath and then laughed and hugged me back and gave me a proper kiss. I knew in that moment that everything had changed for us.

He let me go with much reluctance, but Will was rousing so Harrison and Andre hauled him upstairs to the apartment before he was fully awake and able to fight back.

"We should probably go join them," Viv said. She sounded reluctant and I imagined she couldn't be looking forward to facing her husband, who actually wasn't. Probably, I needed to tell her that.

"Just give me a second," I said.

I ducked back into the open car and searched the front for a latch for the trunk. Finally, I heard it pop. I hurried to the back of the car and lifted the trunk. An automatic light came on and I could see a small wooden crate swaddled in some old blankets.

"That's the Renoir, the real one," I said to Viv.

"You're joking," she said.

"Nope." I shook my head. "Come on, let's get this one and the forgery up to the apartment so the police can see exactly what those two had planned."

It was one of the longest nights in the history of long nights. We didn't get back to Suzette's apartment building until the sun was rising. It almost felt as if we were in a race to beat the first rays of dawn. We lost.

Viv took a power nap and then went to teach her class while the rest of us slept in and woke up to a late breakfast, which we spent recounting the night's events to Suzette. She was a wonderful audience full of outrage and anger on Viv's behalf, distress and anxiety on mine, and then triumph that the police were going to charge Will and Colette with the murder of Jacques Reyer along with a whole lot of theft and fraud charges.

"What about the Renoir?" Nick asked. "Has anything been decided?"

"I heard Inspecteur Lavigne say that once it is no longer a piece of evidence, and the French move fairly quickly on these sorts of things, then the Musée de l'Or will have the opportunity to buy it back from O'Toole Insurance for the cost of the original payout."

We all agreed that this seemed only fair. Marie Brouillard had been brought in for questioning because while it was William and Colette who had stolen the piece this time, it had been taken from the Brouillard estate, which meant that Marie had some things to disclose, such as what pieces her mother had stolen back from the museum, where they were and how much Marie had known about her mother's scam. I suspected Marie knew more than she would admit to and I figured she'd have to sell her estate in order to hire an attorney to prove it. It was going to be interesting to watch the drama unfold.

Alistair had informed us that Colette and William had already turned on each other under questioning by the

Paris police. Each said that the other had been the mastermind behind the art theft, while Colette claimed that she was an abused wife and William had forced her to kill Reyer and William pleaded ignorance of it all, saying that he had no idea his wife was a killer and an art thief. Needless to say, I had told the police all I knew and submitted a written statement and an offer to testify as well.

It never ceased to amaze me how far a criminal would go to avoid working a regular job. Truly, it boggled. But all was well that ended well, except for Jacques Reyer, in the case of the yellow door, or the missing husband, or perhaps we could call it a tale of two paintings. Either way, the mystery was solved and I, for one, was very relieved. Mostly, because I was still alive to tell the tale.

The Paris School of Art always held an exclusive art show at the session's end. It was also a fund-raiser for the school, which made it well attended by those who wished to see and be seen at the high-society affair.

Viv's class had decided to have a fashion show to showcase their work. There was a catwalk going down the middle of the school's art gallery, and one of the ladies had loaded some serious strut music on her mobile phone so the students could walk down the runway to a beat.

"I'm not too late, am I? I didn't miss it yet, yeah?"

I turned around to find Viv's millinery intern, Fiona Felton, standing behind me.

"Fee," I cried and jumped up and gave her a hug.

Tall and lithe with dark skin, dark eyes and a head full of corkscrew curls that presently had streaks of sunshine yellow in them, Fee was a stunner. She was also a heck of a milliner and had gamely minded the shop while we were in Paris for Viv's class.

"It's so good to see you," I said.

"Given what almost happened to you, I have to say the same," she said. She hugged me again, really hard. "You're terrifying, you know that, right?"

"That's what I keep telling her," Harrison said.

He and Fee exchanged hugs and then she moved on down the line to Nick, Andre, and then Alistair, who had not left Viv's side since Will and Colette had been hauled off to jail. I had a feeling from the way they kept looking at each other that something wonderful was happening between Viv and Alistair, but of course, I didn't press because Viv being Viv we'd find out about her and Alistair when she was good and ready and not a nanosecond before. Then Fee hugged Viv and took the empty seat beside her that Viv had saved for her.

We sat back down and I noticed that Harry had his arm along the back of my chair. It was a very "we're a couple" sort of move. I wondered if I should call him on it, but then the show began and I forgot. Okay, I let myself forget. I just had a near death experience, so shoot me, or rather, don't.

Viv's students took turns strutting down the makeshift catwalk. My favorites were the two elderly sisters from

Massachusetts. They didn't strike me as the types who liked to leave their zip code so I got a real charge out of Ella and Marie Porter, especially when they struck a pose for Andre, who had volunteered to photograph the event for the school.

One of the sisters had created a huge yellow bucket hat with a waterfall of yellow feathers cascading down the back while the other's was a shade of kelly green that made my eyes water up, but she carried it off magnificently—in other words, with a lot of attitude.

Lucas Martin was standing off to one side with Suzette. They were both applauding the students, and Suzette actually put her thumb and index fingers in her mouth and let loose an earsplitting wolf whistle, which made Lucas laugh out loud.

"This is pretty great," I said to Harry.

He nodded. Then he looked at me with his bright eyes and said, "I'm really glad you're here for it."

"Me, too," I said.

We hadn't spoken much about Colette and Will's plan to shove me in front of a bus—wow, that expression had a new meaning for me—but it was there.

The possibility of me not being here anymore, of not having a chance to be with Harry, ever, had shifted my priorities dramatically. Suddenly, promises to myself and my mother, vows of celibacy, proving myself capable of being alone, didn't really mean as much as the possibility that I might have lost the chance to tell Harry how I feel about him.

What was the point of being good at being alone if it meant I was constantly pushing away the one person I wanted to be with? In fact, it seemed rather stupid at the moment, actually. And I was tougher than I looked. I could handle my mother's teasing, especially if it meant I got to be with Harry sooner rather than later.

"Harry, I need to tell you something," I said.

He looked at me with a small smile and said, "Really? Because I need to tell you something, too. Something that became very clear to me when I thought I might lose you. Well, that's not true. It's something I've always known but now it seems fairly urgent that I tell you."

"Oh?" I asked. Oh, man, was he in the same place as me? Was he going to tell me he loved me? No, no, I wanted to go first! I felt like he deserved that, given that I had been holding him off for months. I took his hand in mine and said, "Okay, but me first."

"All right, then," he said.

He was looking at me with an intensity that made my heart hammer triple time in my chest. Oh, man, I really needed to get this right.

"The thing is, Harry, that I'm in l—"

"Scarlett? Scarlett Parker? Is that you?"

That voice. It was like a bucket of ice water being dumped on my head. The last time I had heard it, I was throwing fistfuls of chocolate cake at the face hole it came out of. I whipped around in my seat and froze.

There he was, the lying, cheating rat bastard who had caused me to flee the state of Florida and the United States of America in an epic walk of shame, and he was walking straight at me. Looking as gorgeous as ever with his wavy dark hair and deep, soulful eyes, his square jaw and broad shoulders, was my former boss and boyfriend, Carlos Santiago.

"Oh, my God," I said. "It's the rat bastard here in Paris! What are the odds?"

Harrison jumped to his feet. He looked furious and he growled, "That's the spoon who lied to you about being married? The one who humiliated you?"

"Spoon?" I said with a startled laugh. "Did you just call him a spoon?"

"Yes, it's a person too stupid to be trusted with a knife or fork," he said. "And if he didn't treasure you then he is most definitely the dullest of spoons."

That seemed about right. I smiled and nodded as I rose to my feet. Misinterpreting my amusement with Harry as a warm greeting for him, Carlos beamed at me as if delighted to see me. Seriously, if the man had a brain in his head, he would have run for his life. Last time I threw cake at him, this time I wanted to run him through with a hat pin. Apparently, I was still a tad bitter.

"You are as beautiful as ever, Scarlett," Carlos said as he reached me. He winked at me as if we shared some secret special connection. I gagged.

Fury had me bristling as I stood beside Harry. Before it was a complete thought, I was moving out of my row of seats and cruising toward Carlos. The only thought in my head was to slap that smarmy look right off of his face. I was just within striking distance when Harry overtook me. Before I had a chance to register his action, he punched Carlos right in the nose with a loud *crunch*.

Carlos's head snapped back, people shouted, and blood gushed out of Carlos's nose. The gorgeous woman who had been standing next to Carlos, not his wife, shrieked and waved her hands in the air, because that's helpful. Alistair, Andre and Nick appeared beside us. Nick handed Carlos his handkerchief, which Carlos held to his nose as he glared at Harrison.

"Pinch it off and tip your head back," Nick said. "There you go."

"Nice punch," Alistair said out of the side of his mouth to Harry.

"What the hell?" Carlos shouted but it sounded nasal and a bit muffled because of the blood and all. "All I did was say hello, you didn't have to hit me."

"That's for my girlfriend, you rat bastard," Harry snapped. He shook out his fist. "If you ever come near her again, I'll hit you even harder. Am I clear?"

Carlos gave him a wary look and scuttled away with his arm candy hobbling after him in her tight dress and ridiculously high heels.

"Girlfriend?" Nick asked. He turned back to us and his eyes lit up as he savored the word.

"Do tell," Andre said with a grin.

My heart did some weird sort of stutter stop as Harrison turned to face me. In my peripheral vision, I noticed that Fee and Viv had joined our group but I couldn't focus on anyone but Harry. He reached out and cupped my face and then he kissed me.

"Do you remember what I said to you a few days ago when you asked me what I'd do if an ex of yours showed up?" he asked.

Unable to speak, I nodded. I did remember. While we'd been looking for Will that very first day, Harry had been very clear that he'd punch the jerk and then he'd abscond with me. Did he mean it?

"Good, because now that I punched that lousy git, I'm following up on my plan," he said. "I wanted to respect your vow not to date, but I really don't think I can anymore. Come away with me, Scarlett. Er . . . assuming, of course, that you want to."

"Oh, Harry," I said.

My throat was tight and it hurt to push the words past the lump of emotion sitting in there like a brick. He glanced at my face and must have misconstrued my overwrought expression as one of rejection. He dropped his hands and stepped back.

"I see," he said. "Well, that's that then."

"No, you don't see," I said. I laughed as tears dripped down my face, and I stepped forward and grabbed his hands in mine. "I'm in love with you, Harrison Wentworth, and I have been for a really long time."

I heard several sighs, but it was Harry's reaction I wanted to see. His bright green eyes went wide and a grin parted his lips as he brushed the tears from my cheeks with his thumbs. He tugged me into his arms and wrapped me in a hug. Then he lifted me off of my feet so that we were eye to eye.

"I'm in love with you, too," he said. "And I have been since I was twelve years old."

Then he kissed me. So much passion, so much heat, from my proper English gentleman, that if I hadn't already been determined to chuck my no dating rule for him, this kiss would have convinced me. When he set me back on my feet, he studied my face and then he grinned.

"Come away with me right now," he said.

I hesitated. This was it then. My crossroads. The moment I decided which way my life was going to go. Man, I did not want to mess this up. The faint scent of lily of the valley tickled my nose. I glanced at my cousin, Viv. Her blue eyes just like mine, the same shade and shape of our grandmother Mim's, were wide and I knew she smelled it, too. It was Mim, and I knew she was telling me to follow my heart.

"Yes," I said.

And just like that, any silly vows of celibacy or not dating for a year were dusted and done. Harry kissed me fiercely and then tucked my hand through his arm. With a wave to our friends, he led me to the door.

"Where are we going?" I asked.

"For ice cream," he said.

"What?" I cried. "In January?"

"Eighteen years ago, I asked you out for ice cream," he said. "Now I'm going to have that date and if it just happens that we have to take the company jet to a secluded beach on Costa Rica to eat ice cream in an appropriately warm setting, so be it."

"Whoa, whoa, whoa," Andre cried. "Beach? Did you say beach? Listen, I'm not tide down right now, I'll come with you."

"Worst pun ever," I said, ignoring our friends' laughter.

"Quite right, he was just coasting," Viv said. "Take me instead."

"That was awful," I said.

"How about me? I promise I'll come out of my shell," Nick teased.

"Oh, stop," I laughed. "Please!"

"That's right. Give in to the pier pressure," Alistair quipped. "And take me."

"No, no! I missed all of the action, it's my season," Fee chimed in.

"We're outnumbered," I said to Harry.

"Indeed."

"Things have been rough, we should let them come," I whispered.

Harry wrapped an arm around me and asked so that the others could hear, "Are you shore about this, Ginger?"

Their entire group was laughing now, and I looked at all of the faces that were so dear to me.

"Yes," I said. Then I grinned and added, "Let's go make some waves."

The group went silent, their faces blank without a trace of laughter.

"Oh, come on," I cried. "That was a good one. I know you saw what I did there. Costa Rica? Beach? Make waves?"

No one flickered so much as an eyelash, except for Harry. He pulled me in close and kissed me on the lips. Then he pulled back and laughed and the others joined in.

"All right, Ginger, love," he said. "We'll give you that one."

Then he hugged me close and I knew my life was never going to be the same and I couldn't have been happier about it.

Keep reading for a special preview of
Jenn McKinlay's next Cupcake Bakery Mystery . . .

Caramel Crush

Coming April 2017 from Berkley Prime Crime!

“Why are you hiding in the walk-in cooler?” Melanie Cooper asked her friend and business partner, Tate Harper.

“I’m not hiding,” he said.

It was hard to understand him as his teeth were chattering, making a sharp clacking noise that drowned out his words. His lips had a tinge of blue around them and his fingers were shaking so badly, he could barely type on the laptop he had set up on one of the wire shelves.

“Liar, liar, pants on fire,” Mel said. She looked at him and raised one eyebrow. “Bet that would feel pretty good about right now.”

“Wh-wh-where is she?” Tate asked. He blew into his cupped hands and rubbed them together.

“She just left to go look at flowers . . . again,” Mel lied. “Now get out of here before you freeze to death.”

She pushed open the door to the Fairy Tale Cupcakes' walk-in cooler, and shoved Tate out into the bakery kitchen. Mel scooped up his laptop and followed him. The thing was like snuggling a block of ice. *Brr.*

"Sweetie, there you are," Angie DeLaura cried when she caught sight of her groom. "Where have you been? I've been looking all over for you. Sara at the flower shop is waiting for us."

Tate slowly turned and looked at Mel over his shoulder. His eyebrows, which looked to have the beginnings of frost on them, lowered in what she recognized as his seriously unhappy face. Too bad.

Tate and Angie had flipped a coin to see who Mel would stand up for, since they were both her best friends since middle school, and Angie had won, calling "heads" right before the quarter hit the ground. Mel's loyalty now had to be with the bride until the vows were spoken and normalcy returned.

"'To love is to suffer,'" Mel said to Tate. He glowered and she shrugged.

"*Love and Death*," Angie identified the movie Mel had quoted. It was a game the three of them had been playing since they were tweens bonding over their mutual love of the Three Stooges and Three Musketeers bars, because as everyone knows all good things come in threes.

"Well done," Mel said.

"But wait." Angie frowned. She tossed her thick brown braid over her shoulder. "I don't see the relevance. Tate, you're not suffering, are you? You're enjoying planning our wedding, right?"

Mel gave Tate a pointed stare. If he answered this incorrectly, it would be very bad for all of them.

"Of course, honey, I can't think of anything I'd rather do with the sixteen hours a day I spend conscious and breathing than have in-depth discussions on the merits of freesia in the bouquet," he said. Mel noted he had his fingers crossed behind his back.

Angie grinned at him and Mel blinked. Wow, the bride thing must be like wearing a suit of sarcasm-deflecting Teflon, because if anyone else had been on the receiving end of Tate's razor-sharp response, they would be bleeding out by now.

Mel gave Tate a reproachful look. He bowed his head and she noticed his shivering had subsided somewhat. He ran a hand through his wavy brown hair as if to brush off his bad attitude, and when he looked back up, his eyes were crinkling in the corners when he smiled.

"I'd do anything for you, babe, even days and days of looking at flowers, flowers and more flowers," he said. This time he sounded sincere.

"You're the best groom ever." Angie sighed.

"That's because you're the best bride," he returned.

Then he grinned and pulled Angie in close for a smooch. She squealed and then the whole thing turned mushy-gushy, saccharine sweet, and Mel felt her upchuck reflex kick in.

Tate and Angie's wedding was a little over three months away, and if the past few weeks were any indicator, it was going to be a long three months with Angie, who had shocked them all by morphing into a bridezilla who was wholly consumed by her upcoming nuptials and all that went with becoming Mrs. Tate Harper. Truly, it horrified.

Mel was trying to be the supportive best friend, but she really didn't know if she could handle much more of this. Possibly, it was because it was summer in central Arizona, and the heat was making her a little bit crazy. But more than likely, it was because Mel had put off her own wedding to Joe DeLaura, Angie's older brother, so that Angie could have her special day and the waiting was making Mel a bit antsy-pantsy.

Mel and Joe had attempted to elope in Las Vegas a couple of months ago, but because it was Mel and she was sure she was cursed in matrimony, the Elvis impersonator–slash–justice of the peace that her bakery assistant Marty Zelaznik had hired to marry them had turned out to be a fraud, making Mel and Joe's vows worth less than the free limo ride included in the wedding package.

"I love you more," Angie said.

"No, I love you more," Tate replied.

Gag. Mel left the kitchen and headed into the front of the bakery. It was fairly quiet. Marty was restocking the front display case, and Mel blew her blond bangs off her forehead and began to help him.

"Back so soon? I thought you went to bake something," he said.

"I started to get a cavity."

Marty's bushy eyebrows rose up on his shiny dome, and then Tate and Angie came through the swinging door, holding hands and staring into each other's eyes.

"You're beautiful, puddin' pop," Tate said.

"No, you are, snugglupagus," Angie answered with a giggle.

"No, you are, cutie patootie," he insisted.

"Oh, barf on a biscuit," Marty said to Mel. "Those two are revolting."

"Welcome to my world," Mel said. "Honestly, I don't know how much more I can take. Yesterday, they managed three poopsies and two shmoopies in a five-minute conversation and I swear I needed an airsick bag."

"Tell me when they're gone," Marty said.

He shuddered and then turned back to the display case. He looked like he was going to shove his whole body from the shoulders up into the glass case to avoid looking at Tate and Angie as they rubbed their noses together and murmured more lovey-dovey sweet nothings.

Mel was not to be abandoned. She wedged herself in beside Marty and helped him offload the chocolate cupcakes with peanut butter frosting that she had baked fresh that morning. Sometimes in life there was nothing better than chocolate cake with a fresh dollop of peanut butter frosting on top. This was one of those moments.

"Hey, find your own display case," Marty grumbled at her. He nudged her out of the case.

"But this is my display case," she protested.

"I was here first," he argued. "Besides, you're the maid of honor, you have to put up with that."

Mel gave him a look that she hoped clarified how she would not have a problem pelting him with cupcakes until he surrendered control of the glass barricade between them and the sickening bride and groom.

"There are limits to what a maid of honor can manage," she said. "And I draw the line at listening to the two of them call each other—"

"Martin!"

"Huh?" Marty went to stand and smacked his head on the top of the display case. "Ouch!"

Glaring at him over the top of the glass shelving was Marty's current girlfriend, who was also Mel's baking rival, Olivia Puckett, owner of Confections Bakery. She was in her usual blue chef's coat with her gray corkscrew curls bouncing on top of her head in a messy topknot.

Marty rubbed his head as he faced the woman across the counter. He looked wary, she looked irritated, although in all fairness Olivia always looked irritated so she might be as happy as a clam, for all Mel knew.

Mel frowned. Were clams happy? Would anyone be happy stuck in a shell with mostly just a belly, some sinew and one muscly foot for a body? She shook her head. *Focus!*

"Hi, Olivia," she said. "What brings you by?"

"Not the food," Olivia snapped.

Mel pressed her lips together to keep from saying the first thing that came to mind, which was not nice. Her mother had raised her better than that; still, it was an effort.

"Now, Liv," Marty said. "You know we're not supposed to visit each other's place of work. I stay out of your bakery and you stay out of mine."

"Yeah, that'd be fine," Olivia snapped. "Except someone filled up our DVR with reruns of *Magnum P.I.*"

Marty blinked at her. "So?"

"So?" Olivia's arms flapped up in the air like she was trying to achieve liftoff. "I can't record my cooking shows because it's all full of mustache guy."

"Mustache guy?" Marty echoed the words as if she had blasphemed.

Mel ducked back down behind the display case to hide her smile. She noted that Tate and Angie had ceased the PDA and were actively listening to the conversation.

"Yes, mustache guy," Olivia said. "You know, what's his face."

"What's his face?" Marty repeated faintly. He clutched his chest as if he couldn't believe what he was hearing and it was causing him a severe bout of angina. "His name is Tom Selleck and he is a god among men."

"Pish," Olivia said. "He's overrated."

Now Marty staggered back and Mel jumped up to grab him in case he stroked out on the spot. There were few things that Marty held sacred but Tom Selleck was one of them.

"He is not—" Marty began but Olivia interrupted.

"Yes, he is," she said. "So I deleted all of the episodes on the DVR and reprogrammed it to cover just the Food Network."

"What?" Marty cried. He clapped his hands on top of his bald dome as if trying to keep the top of his skull from blowing off.

"You heard me," she said. She looked quite pleased with herself and Mel had a feeling this was not going to end well.

"But . . . you . . . that . . . we . . . I . . ." Marty was so upset he was babbling.

Mel wondered if she should slap him on the back to help him get the words out. There was no need.

"That's it!" Marty shouted. "When I get home tonight, I am moving out!"

Olivia crossed her arms over her chest. She glowered at him. "No, you're not."

"Oh, yes I am," he declared.

"Puleeze," Olivia sniped. "Where would you go? Who is going to take in a man who thinks the floor is a laundry basket, snores like a donkey, and never cleans the bathroom?"

"Says the woman who can't leave a dirty dish in the sink, thinks washing windows is a daily chore, and who writes her name on every single item of edible food in the fridge," Marty retaliated.

Mel met Angie's gaze over the counter. Marty had moved in with Olivia, at her request, just a few months ago. It appeared the honeymoon phase of their live-in period was dusted and done.

"You're impossible," Olivia snapped.

"No, you are," Marty said.

Mel looked at him. As far as comebacks went, that one was pretty lame. He shrugged and turned his back on her.

"Give me until the end of tomorrow, and me and my stuff will just be a fuzzy memory," he said to Olivia.

"Yeah, fuzzy because it's growing mold on it like everything else you leave on the counter," she said.

"That's it!" Marty said. "We're done here."

"We're not done until I say we're done," Olivia argued.

"Too late," Marty said. "Done."

With that, he strode through the kitchen door, leaving it swinging in his wake.

"Hey!" Olivia shouted. "I'm not done with you yet."

She charged behind the counter and followed Marty into the kitchen, where a clang of pots and pans sounded with a bang and a crash. Mel looked at Angie and Tate in alarm.

"What do we do?" she cried.

"Uh . . . nothing?" Tate said.

Crash!

"But my kitchen," Mel said.

She twisted her apron in her hands. More ominous noise came from the kitchen but it did not sound like any more pots and pans were being tossed about.

"Will survive," Tate said. "But you'll never be able to unsee whatever you walk into behind that door."

"I'm with honey badger on this one," Angie said.

"Honey badger?" Tate asked her.

"It's cute," she said.

"If you say so," he said. "I think I'm partial to honey bear."

"How about honey bee?" Angie offered.

Mel blew out a breath. She wasn't sure what was worse, the couple in front of her canoodling or the couple behind her brawling. Either way, she wondered if it was too early in the day, at ten o'clock in the morning, to require an espresso-infused cupcake or two.

The door to the bakery banged open again, but this time a tall, thin woman in a snappy aqua skirt and suit jacket paired with beige sandals and a matching purse strode into the room looking like she was on a mission. She scanned the room and then her deep brown gaze landed on Mel like a laser beam on lock.

A man, also in a suit, came in behind her and Mel had a moment of panic. Was this another couple? Were they looking to book wedding cupcakes? Were they going to be fussing or fighting or goopy in love? She genuinely didn't think she could take much more coupleness, no matter how well it paid.

"Melanie Cooper," the woman said. Obviously, she knew Mel from somewhere. "You're just the woman I need to bake me some break-up cupcakes. Lucky for me, you owe me one, don't you?"

FROM *NEW YORK TIMES* BESTSELLING AUTHOR

JENN MCKINLAY

-The Library Lover's Mysteries-

BOOKS CAN BE DECEIVING

DUE OR DIE

BOOK, LINE, AND SINKER

READ IT AND WEEP

ON BORROWED TIME

A LIKELY STORY

BETTER LATE THAN NEVER

Praise for the Library Lover's Mysteries

"Fast-paced and fun...Charming."

—Kate Carlisle, *New York Times* bestselling author

"A sparkling setting, lovely characters, books, knitting, and chowder! What more could any reader ask?"

—Lorna Barrett, *New York Times* bestselling author